I0549991

BEAUTIFULLY EXPOSED

CANDIED CRUSH #10

CHARITY PARKERSON

The scanning, uploading, and distributing of this book via the internet or via any other means without the permission of the copyright owner is illegal and punishable by law. Criminal copyright infringement, including infringement without monetary gain, is investigated by the FBI and is punishable by up to 5 years in federal prison and a fine of $250,000. Please purchase only authorized electronic editions and do not participate in or encourage electronic piracy of copyrighted materials. Brief passages may be quoted for review purposes if credit is given to the copyright holder. Your support of the author's rights is appreciated. Any resemblances to person(s) living or dead, is completely coincidental. All items contained within this novel are products of the author's imagination.

—Warning: This book is intended for readers over the age of 18.

Copyright © 2020 Charity Parkerson
Editor: BZ Hercules & Consultants
Photographer: Paul Henry Serres
ISBN: 978-1-946099-80-8
All rights reserved.

❀ Created with Vellum

INTRODUCTION

ZEP KNOWS WHAT HE WANTS, AND HE'S POSITIVE IT ISN'T FROST. FROST HAS EVERYTHING ZEP NEEDS.

For years, Zep has been working toward the future he envisions. He wants a husband and kids. Zep knows his worth and isn't willing to settle for less. While Frost is definitely a beauty, Frost is also a liar. He'll never want the life that Zep pictures for himself.

As a former hockey player turned gym owner, Frost is financially settled. He has been known to mislead men occasionally to keep things impersonal, but he has his reasons. Frost also never messes with anyone he could hurt. He never expected to meet Zep.

When Frost's secrets are exposed, Zep sees the man in a whole new light. Unfortunately, as much as they want each other, they can't seem to stay on the same page. Hopefully, they'll figure out a way to meet in the middle. Otherwise, they'll miss their shot at real love.

ONE

TO SAY that Frost was exhausted would be a vast understatement. His muscles felt weighed down by invisible sandbags. He had to keep moving. There weren't enough hours in the day. He had more good days than bad, but the bad days were ugly as hell. Frost had to leave those here at his gym, Fitness Titan. When he had opened the place eight years ago, he had been excited about settling down into a quiet life after years of traveling nonstop while playing professional hockey. Everything about his life had been shifting into a new and positive journey. Now, at forty-one, everything hurt all the time and he was exhausted as fuck. Life was unfair like that.

Frost wound his way through the weight

machines, heading for his office. He kept the place open twenty-four hours a day and only closed on Christmas. Thankfully, he always kept a great staff, so the place ran smoothly. Unfortunately, he still spent more time here than he did at home. It was a good thing he loved everything about working out. For a lot of people, it was a chore. For Frost, exercise was a release he didn't have in any other area of his life. He needed this gym for more reasons than anyone understood. Sometimes, he missed having a social life. Friends. Actually, he missed that a lot. Being an adult was much harder than he expected.

"Oooh, look, Zep. They have water-themed yoga classes."

"I have no idea what that is."

"I think it's basically just regular yoga to the sounds of water or some shit, but how fun."

Frost's head whipped around at the sound of familiar voices. As he set eyes on a pair, he— thankfully—hadn't seen in months, Frost nearly tripped over his feet. Kit was a tiny thing with perfectly styled brown hair and a body that would make any bear want to lick him. The bear beside him named Zep always seemed oblivious to Kit's lickable state. Of course, that was likely due to Kit's unlikable personality. While Kit was a can of kerosene, ready to burn down everyone around him, Zep was floof. Frost didn't really know the pair beyond brief meetings. Kit had ripped into Frost for almost ruining his best friend's relationship. Zep was a regular at a bar Frost visited occasionally. If they planned to join his gym, Frost couldn't avoid them.

He pasted on his most business-like smile and headed their way. "Wow. I haven't seen you two in a while. What brings you to this side of town?"

Two sets of eyes turned his way. A misleading set of sweet-looking browns and an enchanting set of dark blues. Kit's brown eyes narrowed. "Oh, it's the home wrecker."

Zep rolled his eyes, surprising Frost. "Stop, Kit. Jesus. It was all a misunderstanding and it's been months. Let sleeping dogs lie."

Kit turned away and went back to staring at the yoga pamphlet while muttering under his breath. "Yeah. That dog be a lying one for fucking sure."

As if accustomed to Kit's antics, Zep ignored him. "I just bought a house in the neighborhood behind here and was thinking about joining this gym since it's so close."

Frost tried not to look impressed. He lived in the neighborhood behind this place. They were million-dollar homes. Zep looked like a biker daddy. He was easily six-six with a shaggy brown beard and countless tattoos. In fact, he rode a Harley and hung out in a biker bar. The guy did not look like a man who would move into his neighborhood. Not that Frost judged. He too didn't look the part.

Frost's gaze moved Kit's way, wondering if he should ask.

Zep jumped to the rescue. "Kit is here because... we're always together," he finished lamely, as if even he didn't understand why they were always together.

A loud sigh escaped Kit and he focused on Zep. "We're friends."

A smile snapped to Zep's face.

Frost found himself taking a deep breath. Biker daddy was hot.

Zep rubbed Kit's arm, as if comforting a child. "I know."

Kit gave him a sharp nod, as if placated.

Matthew, one of Frost's best personal trainers and the yoga instructor, appeared from nowhere with eyes for no one but Kit. "Hey there. Would you like a tour?"

Kit blindly handed Zep the brochure he had been reading before linking his arm through Matthew's. "Lead the way."

Frost shook his head as the two walked away without acknowledging anyone else.

"Don't mind Kit. He's..."

Frost's gaze met Zep's as Zep visibly floundered for a way to describe Kit. "Mean," Frost supplied.

Zep's shoulders squared. His gaze hardened as much as a softy's could. "He's loyal."

An immediate shot of guilt hit Frost. He had deserved Kit's treatment. Frost shook his head. "You're right. I'm sorry. Would you like a tour?"

A line appeared between Zep's eyebrows. "Do you work here?"

"Actually, I own the place."

Zep's expression cleared. "Oh. That's nice. We see each other occasionally at the bar, but I don't guess we've ever really spoken. I'm Zeppelin," Zep said, formally introducing himself. "Everyone calls me Zep."

Frost shook his hand. "I actually knew that. We run in similar circles. I don't think I have ever introduced myself, though. I'm Frost."

A smile exploded across Zep's face. "I actually knew that, because of all the drama." Damn. Frost would never live down almost accidentally breaking up a couple from the bar. It was a long story, and Frost didn't care to relive it. It seemed Zep had other plans. "Which reminds me. There's something I've always wanted to ask you." Frost held his breath. He didn't want his mistakes dredged up again. Frost was far from perfect. "Who names their kid Frost?"

A laugh burst from Frost without his permission. "This is L.A. Everyone here would name their kid Frost. Who names their kid Zeppelin?"

"Hippies," Zep answered without missing a beat.

Frost couldn't stop smiling. He also couldn't resist being honest. "In my case, Frost is actually my last name. I played pro hockey until I retired eight years ago. All the players get called by their last names and it just stuck. My name is actually John Michael."

Zep winced. "Two first names? Yeah. Frost is better."

Another laugh burst from Frost. "Damn. A guy named Zep just keeps insulting me."

With a smile, Zep made a sweeping motion. "Let's start that tour before you decide to ban me before I can join."

It felt good to smile. In fact, it felt pretty great to be in Zep's company. Frost hoped he could wow Zep so he could see the guy more often.

"I wonder where Kit disappeared to."

Damn. Frost forgot Zep came as a pair. The

sacrifices he made in the name of friendship never seemed to end. It looked like he would have to wow Kit too. That was likely impossible.

WHILE ZEP HAD MET FROST ON OCCASION AND thought more than once the guy was incredibly gorgeous, Zep was a little too impressed today. Several months back, Frost had shown up at Zep's friend Damon's house, started stripping, and almost wrecked Damon's entire life in the process. It had been a huge misunderstanding. Frost and Damon had been sleeping together now and then before Damon started dating his now husband Lucky. Unfortunately, Frost hadn't known Damon was no longer on the market and things had quickly gone downhill. All that drama was easy for Zep to brush away as a gigantic miscommunication. What Zep couldn't understand was what he had learned later.

It turned out Frost had been lying to Damon the entire time they had been sleeping together by claiming he worked out of town. Frost did not in fact work out of town. He owned this gym in the same town where they all lived. He just hadn't wanted a relationship with Damon. It was a mess. The craziest part of all was Zep genuinely liked Frost. Zep was also a bit tender-hearted and wanted to like everyone. In this case, though, Frost was beautiful—like jaw-dropping, make Zep's heart beat a little too fast, hot as hell. Everything from his dark hair to his light eyes and gorgeous body took Zep's breath. They had made eye contact one time at the bar and Zep hadn't forgotten that shot of electricity since. In fact, he sort of kind of knew this was the gym Frost owned before showing up here. He just hadn't wanted Kit to know, so Kit wouldn't shut down his plan to come here. Kit was loyal and explosive. Lucky was Kit's friend. It was still possible Kit might claw Frost's eyes out before the end of the day. There was never any telling with Kit. He might go either way.

Zep listened to Frost talk about boxing classes and different yoga experiences. He eyed the weight room and nodded along as Frost spoke. Truthfully, he didn't absorb a word Frost said. He already knew he would join. The place was convenient to Zep's new place while his old gym was on the other side of L.A. There was nothing convenient about driving to the other side of L.A. and Zep wasn't exactly drowning in free time.

"I can set you up with a two-week free pass if you'd like to try out the place before signing up."

Zep kept smiling while trying to ignore his shallow breaths. "Sounds great."

Frost motioned for Zep to follow him. "Let's head back up front then."

Zep's gaze automatically dropped to Frost's ass the instant Frost turned his back. Good lord, it was perfect. Round and firm-looking. Zep's mouth watered.

"Don't you dare."

At Kit's yelled words, Zep looked away from Frost's ass so fast, he nearly gave himself whiplash. His guilty gaze turned toward the sound of Kit's voice. Kit was leaned against a nearby machine, openly laughing at something with the guy giving him a tour. Zep swiped his hand across his eyes as he realized Kit hadn't been talking to him. He shouldn't be looking at Frost like his next meal. Kit would eat him alive if Zep pursued this. He tried stiffening his spine. Frost was off limits.

"What are your plans after this today?"

Zep met Frost's gaze at the question. He felt like he was falling into Frost's gorgeous light blue eyes. "I'm sorry. What?"

Frost smiled, making matters worse. "You said you moved into the neighborhood behind here.

That's where I live too. Are you headed home, or do you have big plans with Kit?"

"We're not dating." As the words left his lips, Zep's cheeks heated. He had no idea why he had said such a horrifying thing.

Frost didn't seem to notice Zep's embarrassment as he led Zep into an office. "I figured as much with the way he's flirting with Matthew out there. You're obviously a nice guy, but no one is nice enough to put up with that." He motioned for Zep to take a seat.

Zep chose a chair on the opposite side of the desk as Frost sat and started typing on his computer. He tried to act as if he hadn't said anything humiliating. "Yeah. Kit flirts with everyone. He's young and single."

Frost flashed him a smile. "Not to mention he poses nude for a living and is extremely hot."

That hurt. Zep had to take a second. Yeah, Kit was the sexy one in their friendship. Zep was used to not getting noticed, but this one time, it would have been nice if Frost hadn't mentioned Kit's looks. For a moment, it had been nice having Frost's attention. He swallowed the bitterness. "Yeah. There's that."

Frost kept their conversation going without

looking Zep's way. "It's too bad he's not nice in the least."

Goddamn. Frost fucked him up. Zep didn't know if he wanted to be jealous or angry. The thing was, Kit wasn't nice in the least. Kit had just sort of adopted Zep as a friend and grown on Zep. Loyalty won out. "He grows on you."

Frost's gaze moved from the computer screen to Zep. "You never answered my question earlier."

Once again, Frost held Zep captivated. "I don't have any plans."

"What's your address?"

Zep swallowed. "Why?"

A smile exploded across Frost's face. "For the trial membership. I need your address."

"Oh." Heat exploded through Zep's face again. "It's one eleven Magnolia Street."

Frost didn't type the address. "Great. It's a date."

Zep was confused as fuck. He had no idea what just happened. "Um, I'm sorry. I'm confused."

"How's eight work for you? I know that's kind of late to eat dinner, but I have to work."

For a moment, Zep sat in silence, doing the slow blink. It sounded like Frost had assumed a date with him, but Zep wasn't sure. He had to get some clarification. "Was that your way of asking me on a date?"

Frost never batted an eyelash. "No. I didn't ask. Asking gives you an out. Kit hates me, so you'll say no. That's not an option. So... eight?"

Despite his best judgment, a smile tugged at Zep's lips. Frost was annoyingly likable. Just like Kit. "Okay. I guess I'll see you at eight."

"Hey. There you are," Kit said, appearing in the doorway. "Are you signing up? Matthew says he's a trainer and yoga instructor here. We totally have to take his class."

Zep took a deep breath and flashed Kit a smile. It seemed all could be forgiven for a hot yoga instructor. "Yeah. I'm signing up."

"Sweet." Kit snagged the chair next to Zep and dragged it closer before cozying up next to Zep. "They let you bring a friend for free."

Zep rubbed his forehead. Kit was ridiculously good at getting a free ride. "Of course." It looked like he would be taking some yoga classes, because that was what all guys his size loved to do.

As if reading his mind, Kit patted his arm. "It's okay, sweetie. You can just sit on the mat and do breathing exercises. It's yoga. They don't actually force you to do anything."

Zep met Frost's stare.

He must have looked as dejected as he felt, because Frost visibly tried biting back a smile. "He's not wrong. Some people just stay in shavasana to de-stress."

"Great." Zep sounded every bit as miserable as he felt. He had no idea what Frost was talking about since he had never done yoga a day in his life, but it sounded a lot like he would get to be the bored one for half an hour.

For a moment, Frost held his stare. Once again, Zep was back to feeling swept away by Frost's seemingly peaceful presence. An understanding smile touched Frost's lips. "I'll do it with you the first time, so you don't feel awkward."

A breath of fresh air filled Zep's lungs. That was... nice. Zep was used to Kit roping him into uncomfortable things. Frost's offer was a pleasant change. "Thank you."

Something unnamed but oddly sweet passed over Frost's features before he went back to filling in Zep's information. Zep had no clue what happened to his life in the last fifteen minutes, but he felt strangely hopeful. It had been a long time since he'd met anyone nice. He looked forward to seeing if this new thing went anywhere. It was possible they would have an uncomfortable dinner and then would never speak again. If so, that was fine. Zep didn't have a lot of time to waste. He wasn't getting any younger and he wanted a family. The idea of that scared a lot of guys away. Zep couldn't afford to care. He was looking for his unicorn. The one guy out there for him. Likely, Frost wouldn't be the one, but Zep wouldn't pass up his chance to find out.

TWO

TO ZEP'S SURPRISE, at exactly eight, Frost showed. It was as if he stared at his watch and waited to ring the bell until the designated time. With a nervous flutter in his gut, Zep opened the door to find Frost holding an insulated pan.

"This is from my mom."

Zep bit his bottom lip, trying not to smile like an idiot. "That's very nice of her." He took a step back so Frost could pass. The scent of delicious food overcame him as Frost brushed by him. "What is it?"

"Low carb lasagna."

So the smell was deceiving. "Wow." Even Zep heard the question in his tone.

A sexy rumble of laughter fell from Frost's lips to caress Zep's ears. "I promise that you'll love it." Zep motioned for Frost to follow him to the kitchen, and Frost kept up his end of the conversation. "After you left this afternoon, she called, and I told her about you moving into my neighborhood and us getting together tonight. She was adamant that I bring you this and that we stay in and relax."

Since Frost had been setting the pan on the counter while dropping that last bit, Zep didn't get a look at his expression to see how Frost felt about staying in. Zep decided to be honest in hopes that Frost would be as well. "I'm grateful for her. To be honest, between work, unpacking, and spending time with Kit, I'm exhausted." They worked together seamlessly as they spoke, gathering plates, silverware, and drinks.

"I can imagine Kit is exhausting as hell."

A laugh burst from Zep as he chose a seat at the kitchen table. "You have no idea. He's a tiny ball of endless energy. Neither of us work nine-to-five jobs, so I guess we kind of gravitate toward doing things together, except he's—"

"I'm sorry," Frost said, cutting him off. "I'll let you finish that thought in just a second, but while I have you sitting down. You're ridiculously tall, so it makes it impossible for me to do the one thing I've wanted to do for a very long time." That was all the warning Zep got before Frost swooped in and kissed him. There was no warming up or sweetness to Frost's kiss. He went all in, leaving no room for doubt of his intentions. His tongue was in Zep's mouth, stroking and seeking. Zep's breath disappeared as heat blasted him, making him grateful to be sitting. Frost bit Zep's bottom lip and then sucked it in apology. Zep gripped the edge of the kitchen table and held on for dear life. His dick was hard. His body was on fire. He had no clue how he ended up in this position, but goddamn. Zep wanted Frost.

Frost pulled away and sat—like nothing happened. "I know what Kit does, but I don't think I've ever heard what you do for a living."

Zep dropped his gaze to his food for a second and unnecessarily rearranged his silverware to hide the way he felt. If Zep were being honest with himself, he never expected Frost would have any genuine interest in him beyond being friends. He felt like they didn't match. Like they were a before and after picture. Zep looked like what happened to a person after forty-two years of not having enough time to take care of himself. Frost looked the exact opposite. That reminder had Zep mentally shrugging off their kiss. There was no way Frost was doing more than playing with him. He would play along for now.

"I'm a doula." Zep wanted to pat himself on the back for sounding so unaffected until he met Frost's stare. Frost did not look unmoved. His face was flushed, and his eyes burned with lust. Zep's self-preservation melted away. Frost wanted him. Zep couldn't look away.

"I don't know what that is, but it must pay really well," Frost said, motioning at their surroundings.

Zep tried desperately to pull coherent thoughts together into words. "The house is simply good planning on my part. I bought a great house in an up-and-coming neighborhood fifteen years ago on a fifteen-year mortgage. By the time I paid off that house this year, it was worth four times what I paid for it, which covered the cost of this house. Most of my clients are in this area, so I wanted to be on this side of town for convenience's sake. A doula delivers babies in a nontraditional setting. Mostly home births."

Frost's eyebrows raised. "Wow. That's amazing. Does that mean you like kids?" Frost took a bite of his food while waiting for Zep's response.

For a moment, Zep couldn't focus on anything but the way Frost's jaw moved as he chewed. He was such a beautiful man. Zep had to force himself to stay on topic. Thankfully, Frost had given him the perfect opening to let Frost know he had no plans to fuck around with a player. "I adore kids. My entire life, I've had plans of owning an enormous house, getting married, and filling the place with kids. Kids are great." Zep got carried away, losing himself in the dream he hadn't achieved. "They're just these miniature people with tremendous personalities that haven't been squashed by reality yet. They still think the world is massive and beautiful. Truthfully, the world is brighter around children." Zep's smile slipped away. "That dream just never happened for me. I have the house now, but that's about it." Zep shoved a bite of food in his mouth to hide the bitterness of his confession. He really, really wanted that dream. It stung to know it likely wouldn't happen at his age. Surprise jarred him from his depressing thoughts. "Holy crap. That's delicious. I wasn't expecting anything low carb to be this good."

Frost chuckled at his reaction. "Mom has diabetes and has gotten really good at making meals that don't lose flavor for carbs' sake."

"I need to get this recipe from her." Zep happily took another bite while Frost watched.

A sweet-looking smile touched Frost's lips. "I'm sure she'll be more than happy to pass it along."

Frost's staring was starting to make Zep self-conscious. Zep motioned for Frost to talk. "You know my story. Now tell me yours."

To Zep's surprise, Frost looked somewhat uncomfortable at the question, as if he didn't like talking about himself. "You know it. I retired from hockey and started a fitness center. That's pretty much it. I haven't had a lot of time for much else, which really kills the dating scene. No one wants to hear that you have dreams."

Zep nodded. He completely got that. The men he tended to meet didn't understand his drive to do what he did for a living. They didn't want kids or to settle down. The men Zep met wanted to plow their way through as many guys as they could before falling dead of exhaustion and disease. "We live in depressing times for hopeless romantics." A blush touched Zep's cheeks and he dropped his gaze. He always said too much. It was no wonder no one wanted to date him.

Damn. Frost loved watching Zep blush. The guy did it a lot, but Frost pretended not to notice. He didn't want to make Zep uncomfortable, but then again, he kind of did, because Zep's blush was adorable. Every detail he learned about Zep further proved how mushy the guy was on the inside. Frost had no idea what a doula was beyond Zep's description. It might have been a doctor or just a birthing coach. Either way, Zep's profession said everything about him. He was adorable. Frost couldn't decide if he wanted to keep making Zep squirm or push him over the edge. That kiss... wow. Frost had only meant to steal a quick taste. He simply wanted Zep to understand his intentions. The second their lips met, Zep had exploded into passion. There was a lot of hidden hunger in this one. Frost wanted to watch Zep come unglued.

"I won't keep you late tonight. Moving is exhausting, and I'm sure Kit has been zero help." A laugh burst from Frost as another thought hit. "You know, in a way, you already have an unruly teenager. He might not be the kid you crave, but he's the one you got."

Zep huffed. "How old do you think I am? I'm only..." Zep appeared to mentally do the math. His shoulders fell. "Yeah. I guess I am old enough to be his dad, but still."

Frost couldn't stop smiling. "Don't look so crestfallen. I imagine we're really close to the same age. Here. I'll even go first. I'm forty-one."

For a moment, Zep stared at him in silence before looking even more crestfallen. "Are you joking? I'm forty-two and I look at least ten years older than you."

Frost's smile disappeared. "No. You don't. I'm not sure you're seeing yourself, if that's what you think. That happens sometimes when we don't surround ourselves with people who lift us up. It's never good to have only your thoughts to judge yourself with."

Unexpectedly, Zep blushed again. "You're really nice. I wasn't expecting that."

Frost couldn't balk. What Zep knew of him consisted of Frost's near miss at home wrecking. Still, Frost wasn't in a position to actually date anyone. No matter how much he liked them. He also didn't want Zep to be uncomfortable in his company. "How about I help you wash these dishes and then I'll let you relax?"

"It's literally two plates. I think I can handle it,

but you don't have to run off. This is the most relaxed I've been in ages."

Frost stood and carried his plate to the sink. "Only if you're sure. I don't want to overstay my welcome."

Zep flashed him a smile as he set his plate on top of Frost's. "I'm sure. Maybe I could give you a tour. I haven't gotten to show off the house to too many people yet. Kit, of course, and Lucky stopped by yesterday."

At Lucky's name, Frost tried not to flinch. Damon had never meant anything to Frost, but they had been sleeping together for a while. Anytime Frost had a night off or life started suffocating him, he had called Damon, hoping for relief. It seemed strange now that Damon was married. He tried not to show any emotion. "How are Lucky and Damon anyhow?"

Zep led Frost to the informal living area. "The living room. They're good," he said as he headed down the hall, obviously expecting Frost to follow two conversations. "First floor guest room." He kept going. "First floor master. They've got a surprisingly good crew manning the bar now, so they're headed to some tropical destination with Tobin and Sergio for a while. I don't remember when Lucky said they were returning. I feel like it's a solid three months from now, or something similar."

That was nice. Damon had always thought of Tobin as a son, so that was probably good for his mental health to get that much time with him. Now that he had heard too much about everyone else's happy life, Frost felt a hint of the usual depression creeping in. "I hope they have a great time. Your place is set up just like mine. I'm only two streets over on Poplar."

The way Zep eyed Frost had Frost ready to bolt. "There's something I've been wondering since all that stuff happened between Damon and you."

Fuck. Frost did not want to have this conversation. He couldn't explain why he lied about working out of town. It was best he left now.

Zep didn't wait for Frost to agree to the topic. "What sent you running to Damon that night?" Frost blinked. He had not been expecting that question. Zep wasn't done. "I mean, it must have been pretty bad if you didn't give him even five seconds to tell you about Lucky."

No one understood the choking darkness. The anger and resentment. Frost wouldn't explain it now. "You're gorgeous."

Zep looked away, as if disappointed by Frost's

compliment. "All you had to do was tell me it was none of my business."

It hit Frost. Zep genuinely didn't realize how sexy he was. Frost saw him. While standing in the doorway of Zep's bedroom, Frost noticed everything about Zep while standing entirely too close to Zep's bed. "I was being completely serious. You should tell me to leave."

Zep's gaze slid back Frost's way. "Why?"

Frost didn't bother toning down his interest. "We're standing entirely too close to your bed for you to be such a temptation."

With a sigh, Zep turned off his bedroom light and headed back toward the living room. Frost didn't understand Zep's reaction at all. "Tell your mom I said thank you for the lasagna. I'll make sure she gets her pan back."

It seemed Frost was being asked to leave after all. He scrambled for a way to stay in Zep's good graces. He didn't know how to deal with someone who didn't accept compliments. "It looks like you still have a ton of unpacking to do. Would you like some help?"

Zep turned, looking genuinely taken aback by the offer. "Why would you want to do that?"

Frost shrugged, trying to look innocent. "That's what friends do."

A moment passed with Zep staring at him, as if trying to figure out Frost's game. Finally, Zep shook his head and motioned for Frost to follow him. "Come on. The movers stacked a bunch of boxes in the garage. I can only get my motorcycle in there right now, but I'd love to be able to actually park my truck in there too."

Frost tried hiding his triumph over Zep letting him stay. "Oh, yeah. We should definitely get that squared away." Frost couldn't help but smile as Zep turned away. Zep was as good as in his bed. He just didn't know it yet.

FROST WAS WAY TOO FREE WITH HIS compliments. While Zep absolutely knew his worth, he also knew he didn't attract men like Frost. Personally, Zep didn't have a type. Whoever caught his eye, caught his eye. But men who were fitness nuts weren't the ones who came looking for Zep. Zep wasn't massively out of shape. He went to the gym. Zep just had too much else to do to focus all his attention on his body. Plus, life was too short to skip dessert. Zep was thick. Some might call him bear-like. He was fine with that, but still. Guys like Frost were not into guys like Zep.

Since Frost seemed to genuinely want to help and he jumped right in there, unpacking boxes alongside Zep, Zep let it go on. The longer Frost stayed; the more Zep's guard slipped. Frost was nice, funny, and smart. The guy seemed to be the total package. That was terrifying because Zep knew too much. He hadn't forgotten the massive lies Frost had told to keep Damon as only a fuck buddy. The thing was, Zep already knew more about Frost than Damon had. Zep found himself making excuses for Frost. Damon obviously hadn't wanted to be more than friends with benefits, or he would have asked more questions, right?

Zep couldn't stop asking questions. The more Frost revealed, the more stories Zep wanted to hear. By the time they cleared out enough boxes for Zep to get his truck in the garage, Zep knew a ton about Frost. He knew Frost's mom was a nurse named Helena. Frost had a younger sister, Lori. His sister worked at some country club. Her husband, Joe, worked at the DMV. Frost's dad had passed away last year after a battle with colon cancer. Damon should have known those things. Why didn't he ask?

That was such a dangerous thought. Zep was smart enough to see the truth. He liked Frost, and he wanted to believe Frost genuinely liked him. That didn't mean Zep wouldn't guard his heart.

Side by side, they leaned against Zep's kitchen island and drank a bottle of water. Frost finished his first. His gaze skirted the kitchen. "I know damn well a guy like you has a recycling bin."

A laugh burst from Zep. "Yeah. It's behind that door."

As Frost moved to throw his bottle in with the plastics, Zep couldn't take his eyes off him. He was so incredibly gorgeous, and he was like an actual adult. Zep didn't get to spend time with many people his age who acted their age. That was his fault. He had a choice in the matter, but this was nice. It was more than nice. Frost made Zep's longing for a husband twice as powerful. He wanted this life. Zep craved having a helpmate and friend. A partner. Frost made him hope. Zep hadn't hoped in a long time.

"Now that I've worn you out, I guess you probably have to go."

Frost turned a laughing gaze Zep's way. He closed the distance between them, making Zep's heart beat a little faster. "If you think this little work wore me out, you don't know me at all." Only a few inches remained between them. "You'll have to work much harder to exhaust me."

Zep was a good six inches taller than Frost, but Frost still managed to make Zep feel stalked. He was Frost's prey. Zep wanted to be caught, so he stood still. He didn't blow off the desire in Frost's eyes. Zep made a conscious decision to let Frost start whatever he started with a clean slate. He wouldn't think about Frost's past with Damon. Zep would give Frost a real chance. He saw the moment Frost realized Zep didn't plan to shoot him down. Frost's expression shifted. There was no triumph in his eyes. Zep swore he saw... relief—as if Frost was every bit as tired as Zep was with games. That one hint of vulnerability was all it took. Zep made the first move.

Zep lowered his head. Frost met him halfway. With no thought whatsoever, Zep's hands found their way beneath Frost's shirt as their tongues stroked. He dragged the material higher. His pants loosened at the waist, making Zep realize Frost had been working at stripping him. Zep's body ached to be touched. He felt Frost's pocket buzz. Frost immediately jumped backward out of Zep's hold and pulled his phone from his pocket.

"Crap. I lost track of time. I need to go. It must seem like I'm running out, but it's an emergency."

Zep couldn't stop staring. He heard the words, but all he could see was the flush on Frost's cheeks. They really would have fucked in Zep's new kitchen if Frost hadn't gotten that text. Wow. Zep couldn't wrap his mind around that.

Frost reclaimed Zep's lips before Zep could gather a single coherent thought. This kiss was every bit as hot, doing nothing to cool Zep's lust. Frost pulled away again. "We'll talk. This isn't over."

Zep stood in a wrecked daze as Frost headed for the door. For a solid ten minutes after Frost left, Zep stood there, staring at nothing. He had no idea what just happened. All Zep knew was, he could never, ever tell Kit.

THREE

ZEP: *I need to talk to someone about something. It's something you probably don't want to hear, and I know you're on your trip, but I need a friend. I definitely can't talk to Kit.*

Lucky: *Don't worry about my trip. You can always talk to me about anything.*

Zep: *I kissed Frost.*

Lucky: *WOW! How was it?*

Zep: *I feel really awkward and guilty. I know he caused problems with Damon and you. Plus, he used to be with Damon or whatever.*

Lucky: *Stop. You're overthinking things. We are friends. Frost doesn't seem like a bad guy and he would be lucky to have you, so I ask again. How was it?*

Zep: *Amazing, but now I don't know what to do. Like, I know he did some major lying to Damon and Kit would freaking die.*

Lucky: *Oh yeah. You one hundred percent can't talk to Kit about this. If you like him and you keep your guard up until you know you can trust him, then you should go for it. I'm sure he knows you know about the lies he told Damon. I can't imagine he'll try that same thing with you. Who knows? He might have learned his lesson. People do grow and change.*

Zep: *Thank you. I know it's crazy, but I really like him. I haven't liked anyone in a long time.*

Lucky: *You're an amazing guy. I'm sure he can't resist you. Anytime you need to talk, I'm here for it.*

Zep: *Okay. Thanks for listening and have fun on your trip. Love you.*

Lucky: *Love you too.*

FROST: *I JUST GOT OFF WORK AND I WAS THINKING about our kiss. If you're not busy, I'd love to come by and pick up where we left off.*

Zep: *I don't know who you're used to dealing with, but I don't answer two a.m. booty call texts.*

Frost: *I'm sorry. I had just gotten off work when I*

texted you last night, and I didn't think about the time. Sometimes I forget that not everyone has my crazy schedule. I also didn't mean to make you feel like I was after a booty call. It won't happen again.

Zep: *I guess we'll see.*

"YOGA TIME."

Zep blinked at not only Kit's overly bright mood, but also his extra as hell outfit. He looked like he planned to do yoga, but on a fashion runway. His brown hair was flawless, and he wore a hint of makeup. He had on shorts that left very little to the imagination and a tiny tank top. Kit was always beautiful, but some days he made Zep feel like a cross between a Sasquatch and a swamp monster.

"How are we friends?"

Kit snorted. "Please. You love me. Now get your shoes on. Class starts in ten."

Zep dragged his feet. "The gym is literally around the corner. I think we'll be fine."

Kit smacked Zep's ass. "Come on. Frost will be there. You don't have anything to worry about."

Zep tied his shoes and tried not to sound too interested. "I thought you didn't like Frost."

Kit rolled his eyes. "I don't like what he did to Lucky, and I don't like him personally, but you're not me. You're strong and you know what you want. If he tries to pull any BS on you, I know you'll shut him down. You're an excellent judge of character. Plus, I'm not your mom. If you want to be friends with Frost, that's your business."

"All I just heard was blah, blah, I'll say anything to see the sexy yoga instructor again."

Kit didn't as much as blink at Zep's sarcasm. "Don't be thick. I already have the sexy yoga instructor's phone number. You know I'm not one to play coy."

For a moment, Zep sat paralyzed with the desire to tell Kit everything. Kit didn't play coy. He said his every thought, and that was why they were friends. Sometimes, Zep forgot that was why he enjoyed Kit's company. He never had to worry Kit would lie to him or tell him only what he wanted to hear. Kit was Kit. He was one of a kind.

"We kissed."

"Shut. Up."

A smile snapped to Zep's lips at Kit's shock. It was rare for Zep to do anything shocking. He was boring. Zep stood. "We should go."

Kit held up his hand, stopping Zep. "We've got a minute for this. How did this even happen?"

Zep shrugged. "It just kind of did."

For a moment, Kit stared at him in silence. Finally, he shrugged. "All right. We better get going."

Exasperation had Zep following Kit out the door. "Seriously, Kit. I'm pretty sure I recall you threatening to rip the guy's balls off at one time. Now you're 'all righting' me."

Kit made his way to the passenger side of Zep's truck. "Like I said, I'm not your mom. I've already threatened Frost in every way possible. All those threats still hold if he hurts you."

That was fair. Zep decided to let the conversation go, especially since the last time Zep spoke to Frost, it was in anger. Zep still wasn't over that two a.m. text message. He had already been worried he made a mistake by kissing Frost. Zep felt like Frost proved all Zep's worst fears true with that one text. They hadn't even slept together, and Frost thought it was okay to text him in the middle of the night. Zep had to stop thinking about it. He was getting pissed off all over again.

By the time they made it to Fitness Titan, Zep had —somewhat—let it go. Then he found himself sitting on a yoga mat, feeling out of place and wanting to go home. Suddenly, Zep missed that connection he had felt right before that last kiss. Zep craved being back with someone who got him and didn't make him go to an exercise class so completely out of his comfort zone. Kit had promised no one would make him do anything, but if he didn't, he would be the only one. Everyone else had obviously shown up to do this the right way.

A yoga mat unfurled beside him, and Zep glanced over to find Frost settling down next to him. Frost flashed him a sweet smile a half second before Kit's sexy instructor started the class. Zep only half listened. Frost had shown up for him. It was impossible to stay mad now.

"If you showed up today to let the stress melt away, go ahead and get in corpse pose and let the sound of the rainforest wash over you."

Zep looked Frost's way. He had no fucking clue what corpse pose was. Frost settled onto his back with his legs straight and feet spread. With his arms on the floor at his sides and his palms up, Frost looked relaxed. Zep mimicked Frost's pose. He didn't know if he had the pose nailed, but he didn't feel quite as dumb with Frost at his side. In fact, he felt downright happy. That was definitely new.

Up until Zep walked through the door, Frost hadn't been sure if he would bother talking to Zep again. He liked Zep a lot more than he meant to, but Frost wasn't free to jump right into a relationship with every guy who came along. It was obvious Zep didn't plan to settle for less. He didn't know what would have happened if he hadn't needed to leave the last time that they were together. Frost felt certain the night would have ended in the bedroom. He thought Zep wanted him too, but now he wasn't as sure. Frost wasn't that great at trusting his instincts any longer. People were disappointments.

On the floor, side by side, Zep's fingers brushed his. Zep immediately pulled away, as if embarrassed by the small touch. Frost moved his hand closer, intentionally bumping Zep's hand. This time, Zep didn't move away. A heartbeat passed and Frost couldn't take the suspense any longer. He snagged Zep's hand and linked fingers with him. Zep let it happen. A smile tugged at Frost's lips when Zep's hold tightened. There was an unfamiliar pressure in his chest. His shoulders relaxed as the sounds of the rainforest surrounded them. He could easily fall asleep holding Zep's hand. Zep was a calm person. Being near him made Frost's shoulders relax. He had several years' worth of tension in every single one of his muscles. Frost didn't know how else to hold himself together any longer other than to stay as hard as possible against the world.

He couldn't recall the last time he'd held another man's hand. Frost missed the sensation. The connection. Their yoga class passed in a blink of an eye. Frost noticed Zep dragged his feet cleaning his mat. Even though Frost did too, he didn't think he would get even a moment alone with Zep. Kit was there. As if thinking about him conjured him, Kit bounded over, dragging a smiling Matthew along in his wake. Frost shook his head at the way Matthew eyed Kit's body. Matthew had always had a weakness for bratty boys.

Kit didn't spare a glance for Frost. "Matthew is taking me to lunch, so you don't have to wait on me. Since you're right around the corner, he'll drop me at my car on his way back."

"Okay. Have fun."

Frost found himself focusing a little too hard on Zep's tone. He had never asked what the deal was between the pair. For all Frost knew, they might be sleeping together without strings. Red hot jealousy struck from nowhere. He was sick of being forced to share.

Unfortunately, Frost's mood was ruined, and his temper hadn't cooled by the time Zep turned his way.

Zep had that shy look to him again, making Frost feel twice as possessive. "I guess it's just us. Thank you for showing up to save me."

"I told you I would."

Zep blushed and rubbed the back of his neck. He glanced around the room. "Wow. Everyone cleared out quick."

Frost cast a cursory look around. One half of the cavernous room was used for exercise and martial arts classes, while the other half was set up for boxing lessons. Nothing else was on the books for the room today until the afternoon. Matthew had obviously read the heat between them and closed them inside the empty room on his way out. "It's just you and me... again." He met Zep's stare, letting Zep see his interest. "I like having you alone."

"Why?"

A smile snapped to Frost's lips. "What do you mean why? I like you. You confuse the shit out of me. It's like you don't want to be liked, but really, it's too damn bad. You're nice. I like you." Frost peeled his shirt off and tossed it aside. "We have the room to ourselves. Would you like a free boxing lesson?"

Zep didn't smile or budge. He stood with his massive arms crossed over his chest, looking every bit as suspicious as he should. "Was that a genuine offer or an excuse to take off your shirt?"

A smile tugged at the corners of Frost's mouth. "It's definitely one less piece of clothing we'll have to remove."

Zep's hand shot out. He snagged the back of Frost's neck and hauled him closer. Frost instantly went hard. This was what he wanted. He had been poking the bear to watch him snap. Zep's mouth stopped an inch from Frost's. "Is this what you want?"

"Yes." Even Frost heard the desperation in his voice. He was tired. Frost needed someone to take control.

Zep dropped his hand and took a step back. "Then call me when you're ready to get real. Players are a dime a dozen and I'm getting too old for games. Unlike the men you're obviously used to dealing with, I know my worth and I won't settle for less. Stop wasting my time with this mask you keep hiding behind. When you show me a real man, you'll get one in return."

Frost watched Zep walk away while trying to understand what happened. Every time he thought they were on the same page, they weren't. Anger sideswiped him. Zep was no one. Where the hell did he get off psychoanalyzing Frost? Zep didn't know anything about him. He didn't know Frost's story or how hard Frost worked. Zep didn't know shit. Frost's mood deteriorated by the second. He headed for the boxing area. Frost needed to blow off some steam before he exploded. He didn't have the luxury of falling apart. No one fucking knew him. Zep wouldn't survive five goddamn seconds in Frost's head.

Frost didn't bother wrapping his knuckles or grabbing any gloves. He needed the pain. Frost landed several solid jabs to the first bag he came to. He focused on the vibrations running up his arms as he punched harder and harder. His knuckles split. Frost kept going. Physical pain was nothing. He could do this all day. As suddenly as the rage against life hit, it melted away. His arms dropped to his sides. In a way, Zep was right. Frost hid behind a mask, but not for the reasons Zep suspected. This wasn't what he needed right now.

THE MOMENT ZEP STEPPED OUTSIDE THE GYM and cool air touched his skin, his temper slipped away. Guilt set in. For several minutes, Zep stood there, taking deep breaths of fresh of air and clearing his mind. Zep wasn't a mean-natured person. He believed in peace, tranquility, and karma. Everything he put out in the universe always came back to him. He couldn't leave things the way he had with Frost. Maybe Frost was a liar who thought all men should fall to their knees. That didn't mean Zep had to handle things the way he had. He should have simply said, "this isn't what I want" and kept moving. Damn it. He wouldn't sleep until he apologized.

Zep retraced his steps. Before he made it back to where he had left Frost behind, he spotted Frost closing the door of his office behind him. Zep changed directions. He didn't bother knocking. Zep didn't think Frost would answer right now. Instead, he stormed the room.

"I'm sorry. I shouldn't have..." Zep's words died as his brain caught up with what his eyes showed him. Frost had a tiny dark-haired girl on each knee. The three of them sat together at Frost's desk with the girls destroying his things. Frost looked like a completely different person for a half a second before his expression snapped closed at Zep's intrusion. Zep stood frozen. He didn't know what to do or say. His mouth plowed ahead without his brain. "Have they been in here alone this whole time?"

Frost rolled his eyes. "I know you think I'm a prick, but no. I did not leave my daughters alone so I could play with you. They were in the childcare center. If you're coming in, please close the door."

Zep stepped the rest of the way inside the room and closed the door behind him. He couldn't stop looking at the girls. They had Frost's eyes. His mind raced in every direction before settling on the fact that Frost's knuckles were bleeding. "Do you have a first aid kit?"

"Yeah. Are you okay?"

Zep realized Frost was oblivious to his knuckles. "You're bleeding."

Frost shrugged and pressed his lips to the back of one of the toddlers' head. He didn't move away. Frost looked like he tried drawing peace from his love.

Zep could barely breathe past the lump in his throat. "Where's that first aid kit? I'll clean you up."

Frost spoke against his daughter's hair. "It's on the wall behind you."

With his heart in his throat, Zep moved mindlessly. He unhooked the thick plastic box from the wall before dragging a chair to Frost's side. He kept the contents of the box out of the girls' reach while cleaning Frost's knuckles. He tried not to get any more blood on the girls' clothing than Frost already had. Zep didn't speak as he worked, and neither did Frost. The only sound in the room came from the two girls. When Zep finished, he sat back, and their gazes collided. Zep felt sucker-punched. He had a million questions. There was no good place to start.

Zep found his gaze dropping to the girls. The twins looked just like Frost. They were beautiful.

"How old are they?"

"They turned two last week."

Damn. Zep didn't know how to react. "What are their names?"

Frost held up one girl's arm, making her giggle. "Millie." He held up the other's. "Lily."

Lily focused on Zep. "I have a bear on my shirt."

A smile snapped to Zep's lips. "I see that. He looks soft."

Lily stroked the bear, as if testing Zep's theory. She nodded. "Oooh."

Zep chuckled. He physically ached with the desire to stay right here and get to know them.

Millie decided she wouldn't be left out. "I have-I

44

have a frog on my shoe." She fought to stand on Frost's knee so she could stamp one tiny foot on top of Frost's desk.

Zep couldn't stop smiling. "Those are some awesome shoes. Can I try them on?"

"Yes."

Another laugh burst from Zep as she screwed up her tiny face and focused hard on trying to take off her shoe.

Frost intervened. "Leave your shoes on, baby. Zep's feet are way too big, and your socks are too slick for these floors."

She crawled onto the desk and scooted across the surface as if determined to see Zep's feet for herself.

Zep automatically reached for her so she wouldn't fall. As soon as his hands wrapped around her tiny body, she leapt his way. Zep's gaze shot to Frost. He didn't want to hold the girl without Frost's permission. Frost didn't object. He was busy with Lily, who had obviously decided to take advantage of having Dad to herself. She wrapped her tiny arms around Frost's neck and was telling him some story that made no sense to Zep.

Millie was not to be outdone. She squirmed in Zep's hold, trying to use him as a jungle gym. "I-I have a dog at my grammie's house."

"Really? I love dogs."

"Yeah. It's brown. You have to be nice when you pet him."

Zep was having a great time. "What's your dog's name?"

"Todd."

Lily burst in. "Todd licks my face."

Frost smiled. "Probably because your face is always dirty."

The air left Zep's lungs. Frost looked and sounded like a stranger. This was the real him. Zep had never wanted anyone more in his life. Unfortunately, there was a gaping pit in Zep's stomach, waiting to swallow him whole. Frost had twin daughters at home. Was there a husband hiding there too? Zep's face must have looked exactly how he felt because Frost shifted to his feet.

"Let me take these rugrats back to the childcare center and we'll talk."

Zep didn't really want to give up holding Millie. "Would you like some help?"

Frost shook his head. "It's fine. They love the girls who work here. It's never a battle to get them to stay while I work." He shifted Lily on to one hip and held out his arm for Millie. Millie didn't hesitate to climb from Zep's lap to cling to her dad. "Tell Zep

46

bye." Both girls waved wildly over Frost's shoulders as he carried them from the room.

Zep stared at nothing as he waited for Frost to return. He had no concept of time. There were too many thoughts in his head. Frost hadn't lied to him, per se. Unless there was a husband he didn't know about, then Frost had only omitted a significant portion of his life. Damn. Zep was already making excuses for him. Frost had him fucked up. He didn't know where to go from here.

THE WALK BACK TO HIS OFFICE FROM THE childcare center felt like going to his judgment day. Zep's face. Goddamn. He had looked completely torn—like he wanted to demand an explanation, but he didn't want to fight in front of Frost's kids. Frost didn't know if Zep would still be waiting for him. He didn't know what he would say if he was. Frost had tried hard not to tell any actual lies, but he didn't bring men around his kids. He wouldn't be that parent, introducing every guy he met to his babies. No one would be breaking his babies' hearts by disappearing from their lives. Frost would give them a steady life, even if it killed him.

Still, as he headed back inside his office and spotted Zep waiting, Frost felt the guilt creep back in. Somehow, he was always the bad guy. It never mattered how hard he tried. The moment his gaze collided with Zep's, Frost saw the hurt and fear in Zep's eyes. The truth spilled out.

"A year before I retired from hockey, I started secretly dating the goaltending coach." Frost shut his office door and reclaimed his earlier seat. "I decided to retire early so there wouldn't be any drama after we quietly moved in together. We settled into life together. I started this gym and we started planning a family. After lots of back and forth on the matter, we decided to use donor eggs and my sperm. My sister agreed to carry the baby. Everything was perfect. Until it wasn't." Frost didn't meet Zep's eyes as he spoke. He couldn't see any of Zep's reactions. His own feelings were already too much. "As soon as the pregnancy took, everything slowly changed. It seemed like Scott was never home. Then we found out we were having twins, and Scott pulled even further away. When the due date crept closer, Scott came clean. He had been seeing another of his players and they enjoyed an open relationship I wasn't willing to indulge. The freedom of sleeping with whoever he wanted plus whoever they had together made him a million times happier than being tied to only me and our soon to be kids. Since, technically, the kids weren't his and we weren't married, he was free to skip away guilt free. One month later, I found myself bringing home two tiny preemie babies with little to no help." Frost finally met Zep's stare. "I'm sorry I didn't tell you about them, but I..." There was too much. Frost didn't even know how to finish that thought.

"You're protecting your daughters," Zep said, somewhat finishing Frost's thoughts.

"And myself." Frost couldn't let Zep think he was being completely unselfish. "This wasn't the life I planned, but it's the one I got. I'm not good at... Fuck. I like you, but..." Frost ran his hands through his hair in frustration. He dropped his arms and met Zep's stare. "I don't lounge around on the floor, holding men's hands."

A sweet smile touched Zep's lips. "You did today."

Frost nodded. "That's my point. I like you, but I don't know how to make you believe that after Damon and after this, and I don't have the energy to..." Frustration kept stealing his words.

Zep took Frost's hand in his, while visibly trying to avoid hurting Frost's knuckles. "I like you too. A lot. That's not the problem. I've always been a super good judge of character, and my sixth sense was screaming at me that you were hiding something. I just couldn't figure out what." Damn. Frost really wanted more of Zep. Unfortunately, Zep wasn't finished. "You have two precious little girls. I get that you don't want me around them. I'm rough around the edges. The beard and the tattoos. I get that I'm not for everyone. Even with clients sometimes, they take one look at me and pass on using my services. Having a happy past clientele is what's saved me over the years, so I can keep being me. But you don't know me that well, so I get it."

For a moment, Frost blinked in confusion. "What in the hell are you talking about? I just introduced you to my daughters. You get that I didn't have to do that, right? I didn't have to let you stay. Goddamn. You're a great fucking catch. Why can't you just accept that I'm trying to be with you?"

For a moment, Zep stared at Frost in silence before an adorable blush touched his cheeks. "Oh."

Zep's reaction surprised a chuckle from Frost. "You're adorable. I've never met anyone else who's such a crazy mixture of confidence and complete blindness to their worth. Jesus."

Zep shrugged. "I'm complicated." His expression

immediately shifted to defeat. "I'm really not. The truth is that I like you a lot more than I have anyone in a long time. You're messing with my head. I know my worth, but you're so amazing that I don't know if I'm quite that worthy. Does that make sense? Probably not. I mean, after all, you're you and—"

Frost kissed him. He couldn't resist Zep's special brand of insanity. "My bear looks soft too," Frost whispered between kisses. He felt Zep smile against his lips, driving him to be more ridiculous. He stroked Zep's beard. "Oooh, he is soft."

"You're ridiculous."

Frost stole another kiss. "Keep seeing me."

Zep snagged the back of Frost's head, holding him in place so he could deepen their kiss. By the time Zep pulled away, Frost was breathless. Zep held on to Frost's face. "Only a fool would walk away from this."

That wasn't the least bit true. He had been walked away from before, but Frost would take it. As long as Zep kept giving him a chance, Frost would keep taking them. He needed to give this a shot. For the first time in a long time, Frost wanted to start something new. He was completely terrified.

FOUR

IT WAS HARD, but Zep had eventually let Frost
get back to work. What turned out to be even harder
was waiting for Frost to get off work so they could
spend more time together. Zep hadn't been this
ridiculously giddy in years. Kit's SUV still sat parked
outside Zep's house, but they had spoken through
text, so Zep knew he was okay. That was the most
Zep managed to entertain himself. He got a call from
a patient, but her contractions were only Braxton
Hicks. By the time he made it to Frost's house, he
practically leapt from his truck. He didn't know
where they were headed. Zep couldn't wait to
find out.

Frost's house looked a lot like Zep's, except the
colors were darker. He also had amazing

landscaping. Zep caught a glimpse of a pool in the backyard before heading for the door. Frost didn't give him time to ring the bell before the door opened.

"I saw you on the camera." That was all the greeting Frost gave before snagging the collar of Zep's shirt and hauling him inside the house. Their mouths met as if they had been starving for each other all day. Frost wasted no time trying to divest Zep of his clothing.

"Wait. Where are the girls?"

"My mom's house for the night."

That was all Zep needed to hear. He pulled his shirt up and over his head before tossing it aside. While Zep hadn't come here for this, he was ready. Frost had been in his head all week. Now that he had finally seen behind the mask to the real Frost, Zep had no reservations. He wanted Frost. Frost's short nails scored Zep's skin. He already had Zep's pants unbuttoned and unzipped, massaging Zep's cock.

Zep gently extracted Frost's hand from his pants. "Slow down. Where's your bedroom?"

Frost focused on him with glazed eyes and flushed cheeks. "The same place yours is."

"Let me take you to bed."

Frost blinked, as if his mind was a mess of lust. Zep's knees weakened. He didn't think anyone had ever wanted him as much as Frost obviously did. It was empowering and sexy. Frost's desire hit Zep in the feels. Then Frost decimated him. "You don't understand. I never get to be free."

Fuck. Zep didn't have kids, but he understood. He too was always the responsible one. Zep didn't get to float around, acting like real responsibilities didn't exist. He would let Frost do whatever Frost wanted tonight, but not while standing in the foyer.

"You're about to be as free as you want with me." Zep easily lifted Frost from the floor and tossed him over his shoulder. Frost might be the gym buff, but Zep was bigger.

A loud laugh burst from Frost as Zep headed for the bedroom. He took a cursory look around. He found the king-sized bed and tossed Frost down onto the mattress.

Frost's eyes swam with laughter. "No one has ever pulled that shit with me."

Zep went to work tugging off Frost's clothes. "There are some benefits to being the biggest guy in the room." Zep met Frost's stare. He wanted Frost to see the truth in his eyes. "I can and will treat you the way no one else ever has. Get ready for a lot of firsts."

Frost didn't look away or back down from Zep's

intensity. "You sound a lot like you expect this to be the first night of a full-blown exclusive relationship."

While Zep hadn't expected this important of a conversation to take place right now, he needed Frost to know where he stood. "That's what I want with you."

"Good," Frost said, surprising him. "That's what I want too."

Zep found himself crawling onto the bed, slowing things down. He held Frost's stare as he moved in close. "I definitely think this new deal should be sealed with a kiss. Then I want you to tell me how you like it."

Their lips met. Zep's heart slowed. They had all night. He wanted to make love to Frost. His dick throbbed, but this wasn't about getting off for Zep. He craved the connection. For what felt like forever, their tongues stroked. They savored each other, making out like teens who had been left alone for the night. Their hands roamed until there wasn't a stitch of clothing left between them. Zep worried he wouldn't last long once things really got started.

Frost's mouth moved from Zep's lips to his ear. "Fair warning. I love every act that gets me off. Tonight, I really want to be inside you."

Zep nearly blew. His breathing turned ragged as

Frost's hand slipped beneath Zep's balls and toyed with his asshole. "Can you handle that? Or do you only top?"

"I can handle that." Even Zep heard the neediness in his tone.

A sinister smile touched Frost's lips, as if he relished the thought of what he would do to Zep's body. Frost crawled to the bedside table and rummaged around before coming back with a condom and lube. Zep tried not to squirm while Frost fingered him with oiled fingers, stretching him and driving Zep insane. Since Zep wasn't one of those guys who slept with everyone who came along, and he almost always only met men who saw him as a top, this was an extremely rare experience for him. Truthfully, it had been many years since anyone had wanted him like this. He kept expecting the pain. Instead, Frost was teasing him with pleasure.

By the time Frost settled between Zep's thighs and swiped his crown across Zep's asshole, Zep was ready to scream. He had never been this frustrated and horny. Then Frost was inside him, and all Zep could do was gasp. Frost slowly rocked inside him, pumping at the perfect angle. Zep could barely keep his eyes open. Frost didn't let up from massaging the exact internal spot that stole Zep's thoughts. Then

Frost's thrusts turned to pounding. His lips closed around one of Zep's nipples. He sucked and nipped as he destroyed Zep's asshole and tugged on Zep's cock. There wasn't an ounce of dignity left in Zep. He would have done or said anything for release. Then everything went still inside Zep, as if he balanced on the edge of a knife. For a split second, he saw everything with complete clarity. One of the most beautiful men that Zep had ever seen was inside him and wanted a future with him. His muscles jerked. An orgasm tore through him. Words fell from his lips and Zep had no clue what he said. No doubt it was something humiliating, but Zep didn't care. He was too busy shaking with pleasure. The sound of Frost shouting his name barely penetrated Zep's fog. He fought to catch his breath as Frost kissed him deep. Tiny aftershocks had Zep's dick twitching between their bodies.

Frost's kiss slowed. Their hearts pounded against each other. Zep felt every sensation. He memorized every detail. This had been the best night of his life. It wasn't over yet. He had no clue how to top this, but he would try. Frost said he didn't get to be free. Zep would make him fly.

FROST'S BODY FELT LIKE GELATIN. HE STARED AT his darkened bedroom ceiling with his mind a crazy mixture of calm and whirling. He hadn't expected Zep. Frost hadn't expected to feel this good. He was almost scared of the way his lips wanted to lift in the corners. Zep was the opposite of every guy Frost had ever dated seriously. Back when he played hockey, he dated somewhat within his profession. Trainers. Players. That sort of thing. Honestly, he never pictured himself with anyone long term until Scott.

Scott had stormed into Frost's life and taken over his senses. In a way, Zep had done the same thing. That was why Frost was so terrified. He had let Scott decimate his good sense. It had cost him everything. Frost didn't want to be the same with Zep. Then again, he didn't think Zep was anything like Scott. Zep was sweet until he wasn't. Damn, that was hot. His dick should be dead, but it stirred at the thought of the way Zep had had let Frost fuck him. Yet he hadn't given Frost an ounce of genuine power. He might have let Frost have his way, but Frost had known Zep could take control back any second. Damn. Zep's acquiescence was sexy as fuck. Frost wasn't used to anyone being bigger than him. Yet Zep had manhandled him at the drop of a hat.

Frost pressed his hand to his stomach. Butterflies

stirred. He really liked this new feeling. It felt a lot like happiness. His gaze slid Zep's way. He found Zep watching him. Suddenly, Frost wanted all of him. "What are you thinking?"

Zep didn't smile. His gaze never wavered. He was as solid as ever. "That you're beautiful."

He didn't think Zep meant on the outside. His tone went deeper than that. The butterflies in Frost's stomach stirred to life again. "You sound tired."

"I am but I'm not."

Frost got that. He didn't want to sleep either. He wanted to stare at Zep and dream. Dreams had been lost to him for a long time. "I don't think I've stopped smiling on the inside since we met. If that makes sense."

Zep kissed Frost's shoulder. "It makes sense."

A thought hit Frost, and terror struck right behind it. "I don't want you to lose friends because of me. Kit. Lucky. Everyone will likely have something to say."

Zep's hand encircled Frost's throat. He swept upward, stroking the thick growth of hair on Frost's chin. Words died in Frost's throat. His eyes fell closed in pleasure. Zep always stole his thoughts with his perfectly timed touches. "My friends are real friends. Not only have I already told them I have feelings for you, they all trust my judgment. They're good people. They want us to be happy."

Frost still couldn't open his eyes with Zep stroking him. A chuckle escaped him. "I want to remind you that Kit has threatened my manhood more than once."

"I imagine that threat still stands, but Kit is a rambutan. You have to get past his prickly shell to find the sweetness. Like all of us, life has made him who he is."

Frost met Zep's stare again. "Is there anyone you can't find the good in?"

He felt more than saw Zep shrug. Zep moved closer. "I don't want to live in a world where no one gets a second chance." He swiped his lips across Frost's. "I'm pretty sure my body is dead, but my brain wants more." He kissed Frost again before moving to Frost's jaw and on to his ear. Goosebumps skirted across Frost's skin as Zep open-mouth kissed his ear. Zep shifted positions and moved to Frost's shoulder. "I love this tattoo." Frost's arm was tattooed from the shoulder to his elbow with roses and a clock. "Are you late for a very important date?" Zep asked as he kissed his way to the inside of Frost's elbow.

Frost knew the question was in relation to the

Alice in Wonderland theme of his ink, but the question hit differently with Zep's lips on his body. Maybe he was a little late finding Zep. Perhaps he had done life a bit backward, starting with kids and then finding someone he liked a little too much. Frost regretted nothing at the moment. As Zep's lips landed on his hipbone, Frost's fingers found Zep's hair. His breath slowly released through his nose. Frost savored every sensation.

"I am late," he admitted, even though he knew the words didn't make sense to Zep. "But I'm not giving up."

Frost fully intended to give Zep his all. They were starting something real. He felt that in his bones. Frost wouldn't let anything ruin this.

FIVE

THE SMELL of cooking food and coffee had Zep blinking against his unfamiliar surroundings. It took him longer than usual to gather his thoughts between his move and staying the night with Frost; he was worn out. A smile tugged at the corners of his mouth. He stretched. Memory after memory came back to him, heating his cheeks. He had been shameless. His muscles ached in the best way. He couldn't believe he had demanded an exclusive relationship from Frost and then spent the night ruining Frost's sheets. Zep wanted to text Kit and tell him everything. He wasn't the gushing type, but this was different. Zep didn't have stories to tell. Despite Kit's prickly personality, Zep knew he would listen.

Zep rolled over and sat up. He checked the time

on his phone. It was nine and he had missed a text from Kit. He opened his messages.

Kit: *Hey, I just got here and you're not home. I imagine you're working or whatever. Hopefully, you don't mind, but I used my key to let myself in. I didn't want you to be surprised when you find me on your couch.*

Sometimes Zep worried about Kit. Obviously, he didn't care if Kit came and went. He wouldn't have given Kit a key otherwise. The thing was, Kit never slowed down. Yet he didn't seem to have any direction in life. It was as if he was incapable of sitting quietly with his own thoughts. The idea of that scared Zep. He knew Kit had been through tons of counseling, but some people couldn't be helped. All he could do was keep being Kit's friend.

Zep: *You're probably sleeping now, but you know you're always welcome. I love you. Go ahead and take my bed for now. I'm at Frost's, but when I get home and you're ready, we'll go buy you a bed for the guest room. As long as I have a home, you will too.*

Zep set his phone aside and focused on himself. He needed to find his pants. Frost was obviously making breakfast, and Zep couldn't wait to kiss him good morning. Chances were good that Zep was setting himself up for heartbreak, but he would never know if he didn't try. Onwards and upwards. He wanted to be with Frost.

SINCE THEIR FIRST KISS, FROST HAD KNOWN HE was skating a super fine line. He had known Zep long enough to know the guy had a heart as big as his six-foot-six frame. But Zep also didn't take any shit from anyone. Frost didn't doubt that he couldn't play games with Zep, but he also hadn't planned to introduce Zep to his girls. Until Zep's speech about wanting a house full of kids, that is. That moment had gotten him thinking. Zep had been so passionate and his longing for a family had shown itself in every word the guy spoke. He hadn't been saying what he thought Frost wanted to hear. From his soul, Zep wanted a family. Frost trusted Zep not to hurt his babies. Still, he didn't plan to throw them together very often if he could help it. He needed to take things slow. Zep wouldn't have met the girls yet if he hadn't burst into Frost's office. From now on, he would be slow and steady. This morning was an exception.

"What's this?"

Frost smiled at Zep's laughing question as he

made his way down the hall and inside the kitchen. "The girls and I are making you breakfast."

Both girls wore their tiny aprons and chef hats. Frost had set up a small space at their kid-sized table and toy oven for them to play with a bowl of unusable pancake mix.

"Oh my gosh. This is great." Zep went down onto his knees to see what the girls were doing.

Frost worked on the real batch of pancakes while watching the three of them make a mess. Pressure grew in his chest. He knew Zep loved kids and that was why he chose to play with the twins, but no one understood. This was the life he pictured before Scott left. He had thought this would be their future. Now, here was this guy doing the things Frost had envisioned with a different man. Frost didn't want to dream again. He had already been crushed once in this lifetime. At least, when Scott had destroyed him, the girls hadn't been born yet. They didn't know what they had lost. If they fell in love with Zep and then Zep walked away, the heartbreak would be twice as devastating. He didn't know the right way to handle this new relationship, but he wouldn't pretend his daughters didn't exist. It didn't look like Zep intended to ignore them either.

A laugh burst from Frost as Lily tried feeding

Zep a bite of raw batter that both girls had definitely dug around in. His laughter doubled when Zep ate it without complaint.

"You ladies are doing a fabulous job. I'd recommend your restaurant to anyone."

Frost shook his head. "Okay. Let's get cleaned up so we can eat." As Frost reached for Millie, he stole a kiss from Zep. It wasn't anywhere near the good morning kiss he wanted, but they weren't alone. To Frost's surprise, Zep jumped in to help. He carried Lily to the sink and washed her hands before tossing the hat and apron in the washing machine. While Frost strapped the girls in their booster chairs at the table, Zep cleaned up the kids' work area. Frost barely spoke. He was too busy trying to hide his feelings. Other than his mom and sister taking the girls for overnight visits, Frost never had help. He did everything for them by himself when they were at home. They were his kids. He loved them and being their dad was his job, but it was exhausting work. Frost hadn't dared to dream that things could be different.

The moment they were settled, Zep focused on him. "Thank you for this, but you should've made me get out of bed sooner. I would've helped."

Zep had no idea. He had already been more help

than Frost ever received. "It's fine. Mom had brunch plans, so I had to get up early anyhow. Plus, I have my two helper chefs."

For a moment, Zep stared at him without speaking. He visibly swallowed. "You're so lucky."

Frost had to take a breath. "I know." He had a feeling he was even more blessed than Zep believed because he had Zep with him right now. For the first time in years, Frost wanted to take a chance. He wanted to believe life could be more. Only time would tell if Zep was the one.

SIX

FROST: *Mom can't get here to get the kids before the childcare center closes and I can't leave for another hour.*

Zep: *Don't worry. I'll get them.*

Frost: *Are you sure? That's a lot to ask.*

Zep: *No. It's not.*

ZEP: YOU SHOULD SEE ALL THE PICTURES THE GIRLS *have drawn for you today.*

Frost: *I can't wait. Did you draw me anything? I like gifts.*

Zep: *You'll get my gift when the girls go to bed.*

Frost: *Damn. I miss you.*

Zep: *Same. So hurry home.*

Zep: I'M DROPPING THE GIRLS AT THE CHILDCARE *center. One of my clients is in labor.*

Frost: *No problem. Good luck. Fingers crossed they give this child a normal name.*

Zep: *Not that I can judge.*

Frost: *True, but I love your name.*

Frost: SEND NUDES. I MISS YOU.

Zep: *I'll give you the real thing if you're bored.*

Frost: *Oooh, is that so? Does that mean my sister has picked up the girls and you're free to fuck me in my office?*

Zep: *Yes, the girls are gone. No, I'm waiting for you to get home so I can be as loud as possible.*

Zep: WE NEED MILK.

Frost: *I'll grab some on my way home.*

THE NUMBERS ON HIS COMPUTER BLURRED AS Frost disappeared inside himself. He hadn't wanted to come to work today. All of his well-intentioned plans of keeping Zep from spending too much time with the girls had fallen to the wayside quicker than he ever dreamed. Zep was too good to be true. It seemed like Zep was always there, helping to pick up the slack. Frost didn't know how it happened. One night, they decided to be an exclusive couple. The next thing Frost knew, Zep had a bedroom for the twins at his house and kept them home with him when he didn't work so they weren't always stuck at the fitness center's kid's zone. The four of them did everything together. It was as addictive as hell. Frost didn't want it to stop. Sometimes, he would find himself completely frozen with fear. His daughters would know if they lost Zep. His phone buzzed, pulling him from the sudden terror. He glanced to see an image text from his mom. Frost opened his messages and a laugh burst from him. Zep wore a crown and held a tiny pink plastic teacup. Several fake necklaces draped his neck. Frost's laughter turned into a huge grin he couldn't shake. He studied every detail. Both girls sat with Zep, obviously using him as a jungle gym as they played dress up. Frost found himself responding with the first words that came to mind.

Frost: *He's perfect.*

Mom: *He really is. You did good. I'm picking up the girls for our slumber party.*

Frost: *Okay. Call me when you get home so I can tell them I love them and all that.*

Mom: *Will do. I love you.*

Frost: *I love you too.*

They would be alone tonight. In their six months together, between Zep's job and the girls, they had only had a handful of nights alone. Frost had to take a steadying breath. While Zep's obvious love for Frost's daughters was pretty irresistible, their relationship was the hottest he could recall having. There was nothing Zep wouldn't do. When he was turned on, he went from being Frost's sweet bear to a hulking alpha and it was sexy as fuck. While their sex life wasn't hurting from having to sneak around the kids, the nights they didn't have to hold back were mind blowing. Maybe he would cut out early today so they could make the most of their alone time.

A knock on his open door stopped Frost from texting Zep all the things he planned to do to his body. When he turned his head, all thoughts fled. Six feet of heartbreak stood waiting for his attention. Frost knew his expensive suit hid a body that was sculpted to perfection. His cool blue eyes were focused on Frost, waiting. He smiled when Frost couldn't make his tongue work.

"Hey, Frosty."

Still, Frost had nothing.

Scott looked the same. He hadn't changed at all. Frost felt sick. He fought the urge to flip over the picture frames on his desk, protecting his babies from his ex. Frost wanted to throw things and scream. Scott had no idea what he had left behind. There were so many words that Frost had none.

"I don't even get a hi."

It was like no time had passed. He went straight back to the anger and the hurt. His eyes burned. There was so much rage and bitterness, Frost couldn't think of which hurtful thing he wanted to say first. For the first time in years, Frost had finally found happiness. He finally saw a future for himself. Of course Scott would show up to ruin everything. Frost felt like he should have seen it coming. He wasn't allowed to be happy. Scott would never stand for that. Frost felt like he had already lost Zep.

By the time Frost came through the door, Zep was on the verge of pacing. He had spent the past hour swinging wildly between wondering if he should cook dinner or just strip and wait.

"I see Kit's SUV is parked out front again. Is he here?"

Zep met Frost halfway and claimed a kiss before answering. "He was, but he had a lunch date with Matthew. They never came back. I never know when he'll come and go. He's a free spirit. Your mom picked up the twins about an hour ago."

Zep tried not to tackle Frost to the floor. They didn't get much time alone. Zep wasn't complaining. He loved their life, but their alone time was precious.

"I know. She called me a few minutes ago to let me know she had made it home and so I could tell the girls goodnight."

Frost seemed almost wooden. Alarm bells sounded in Zep's head. "Is everything okay? You seem... I don't know..."

"Take your shirt off."

Zep obeyed. He didn't need to be told twice. All thoughts of there being a problem flew out the window.

Frost stepped closer and ran his hand down Zep's chest. "I don't think I take enough time for you. I don't treat you like you deserve."

Zep's forehead furrowed. "What's..."

Frost dropped to his knees and went to work on Zep's pants.

"You know Kit might come bursting in here any moment."

"Then he'll get a show. This is my house." Frost swallowed Zep's cock before Zep could respond. Zep's fingers dove into Frost's hair. All thought ceased. Frost didn't tease. He bobbed on Zep's dick, sucking and swallowing. All Zep could do was hold on and try to breathe. Zep didn't know if Frost was that amazing or if Zep was so in love that everything that Frost did was perfection. Either way, Zep didn't last long. Before he knew it, his breaths were coming out like shots and the desperation had him pulling Frost's hair harder than he could control. Frost sucked just right, and Zep exploded. His muscles shook. He had to lock his knees to stay upright.

With drops of cum still dripping to the floor, Frost shot to his feet and bent Zep over the kitchen island. There hadn't been a single time in their relationship that Frost had let Zep prepare to get fucked. This time was no exception. Zep never knew it was coming. He was still riding the high of his orgasm when he found Frost's dick in his ass. Zep groped the island tight while Frost fucked him hard with nothing but a lubricated condom to ease the way. Never in all his years had Zep expected to want this rough treatment. Frost made him crave it. Zep couldn't explain it. Frost rolled Zep's eyes back in his head with his hard thrusts. He always found that perfect angle. Zep had just come, and already he was ready to blow again.

Frost bit his back. "I know you can do it, sexy. Paint this floor with cum. I know this tight asshole can squeeze me hard enough to make me hurt all day tomorrow."

Zep white-knuckled the counter and tried to breathe.

"That's it, Zeppelin. I can feel you getting closer. No one knows this body like I do. I know you can pull two orgasms in a row. Jesus. I can still taste your cum. You make me so horny, I want to hurt you for it."

Zep sucked air and then held his breath. His muscles clenched.

"Goddamn. You're going to break my dick off."

Pleasure knocked the wind from Zep. Harsh breaths cut through the air as waves of ecstasy made him shake. Cum hit the kitchen floor. Frost's fingers bruised Zep's skin as he held tight and slammed inside Zep. As Frost cried out, Zep's eyes fell closed. He savored the sounds of Frost's pleasure. Sometimes, they felt like a fantasy. Zep worried he would open his eyes one day and realize they had been a dream. He had been looking for what they had for so long that he didn't know how they could be real.

Frost kissed his spine as his dick slipped from Zep's ass. "Come on, angel. I want to hold you."

Zep's eyes stung as Frost took his hand. Frost tossed the condom in the trash before they headed for the bedroom. At the edge of Zep's bed, they finished stripping away the random articles of clothing they still wore before Frost disappeared inside the bathroom. He reappeared with a wet washcloth.

"Get in the bed, sweetie. It's time for me to take care of you."

Without a word, Zep obeyed. He settled onto his back and Frost gently cleaned him. Zep should have felt embarrassed. He didn't. Instead, peace washed over him as he watched Frost's every action. They had been solidly a couple for just over six months. Neither of them had said they loved the other, but this was love. Zep felt that shit. No one treated someone with this much care unless it came from the heart. He couldn't believe this was anything less than real. As Frost tossed the washcloth aside and settled into Zep's arms, Zep's throat swelled. He had learned something else in the past six months. Frost didn't act like he had tonight unless something about life had him feeling out of control. He also knew Frost wouldn't talk to him until he was ready. All he could do was hold Frost and wait it out.

No matter the reason for Frost's neediness, Zep loved these times the most. He adored holding Frost in the dark and quietly talking or just enjoying the silence together. There was no doubt in Zep's mind that he could see himself doing this for the rest of his life. More times than he could count, Zep had almost broached the topic of their future. Every time, something held him back. He couldn't hear Frost say they weren't forever.

"I got an unexpected visitor at the gym today."

For no reason at all, Zep smiled into the darkness at the sound of Frost's voice. "Good unexpected or bad?"

He felt Frost shrug. "More shocking than anything. It was Scott."

Zep's insides went cold. He knew there were

likely lots of words he could and should say. Nothing came to mind.

Thankfully, Frost didn't wait for Zep to rub two thoughts together and create words. "He wants to see the girls."

"You told him no, right?" Fuck. Zep honestly hadn't meant to sound so angry, but there it was. The twins weren't his and he had no right, but he did not want some strange guy visiting with them.

"Of course."

Zep's muscles relaxed a hair. "Why does he want to see them?"

He felt Frost shrug again. "He said some shit about missing me and realizing how much he lost. Apparently, he panicked or went through some mid-life crisis, or whatever. Now he wants to be a part of the girls' lives and prove he's worth giving a second shot."

The problem was that Zep had always been empathetic and levelheaded. He saw things from other people's points of view. This one time, though. He was torn. On one hand, Scott was who Frost planned to help him raise Millie and Lily. Zep understood that Frost had to consider Scott's offer with an open mind. Then again, fuck that guy. He hadn't been here. Scott had been out there, fucking god only knew who while Frost did everything alone. Zep couldn't believe Scott's nerve.

"You're being awful quiet."

Zep took a breath. He didn't want to say the thoughts racing through his mind. "I'm processing."

Frost's body shook with laughter. "You can say what you're thinking. I likely had all the same thoughts."

"You should let me marry you and adopt the girls. That way, he has no legs to stand on."

A loud snort escaped Frost. He rolled away and covered his face. After a minute of shaking with laughter, Frost's hands fell away from his face. "That was dramatic. Maybe saying you were processing was better."

Zep had been one hundred percent serious. He would marry Frost and adopt the girls in a heartbeat. He was a tiny bit hurt by Frost's reaction to the idea. Sometimes, it felt like they were going places. Other times, Zep felt like he was spinning his wheels. He knew Frost liked having him around, and that this was love, but he wasn't as certain Frost intended to keep him. Zep decided to pretend he hadn't said anything.

"Do you think he could get ugly?"

Frost made a helpless gesture. "Once upon a

time, I would have said no. Now, I know he's capable of anything."

Zep tried calming down. Nothing could or would be done tonight. "Well, whatever happens, I'm here."

Frost rolled back into Zep's arms and settled his head on Zep's chest. "I know. You're amazing. I'm just feeling a bit blindsided, I guess."

Zep snorted. "I'm sure that's an understatement. Do you want me to beat him up for you?"

He felt Frost shake with silent laughter, just as Zep hoped he would. "Thanks for the offer, but no. I'm hoping this was just a fluke. Like maybe he just had a fight with *Jean Pierre* and came running back thinking I'd be an easy mark." The way Frost said Jean Pierre's name left no doubt that he was the other man. It also made Zep realize something else. Neither of them really talked about their pasts. They had jumped into being a full-time couple, practically co-parenting the twins from day one. Life was so hectic that they didn't waste time on the past. They were always barreling forward, focusing on the now. Honestly, he kind of liked that about them. It would be a long time before they heard all of each other's stories. Right now, the girls were little. They were their biggest focus. Nights like these were precious.

"Mom is taking the girls shopping tomorrow and to some play date with her friend's grandkids. They won't be home until around dinner time tomorrow."

Zep felt guilty for how happy that made him. He loved Millie and Lily with all his heart, but he loved Frost too. He wanted more of this.

Frost wasn't finished. "So, I was thinking I should stay home tomorrow."

Zep had to stop himself from squealing like a teenage girl. He forced himself to temper his reaction. "I like this plan. Am I a part of it?"

Frost went up onto his elbow and met Zep's stare. "You're more than part of my plan. You're the whole goddamn thing. All day. You and me. Sleeping, eating, and making love. What do you say?"

"Yay." Zep's cheer came out in a whisper. His throat didn't want to work with all the love sitting on his windpipe. As Frost leaned in and covered Zep's mouth with his, Zep's heart swelled to overflowing. Frost was a dream come true. He was the entire package. Maybe tomorrow Zep would find the courage to admit his feelings. Maybe not. Either way, they would be together. That was enough.

SEVEN

IT SHOULD HAVE BEEN a beautiful day. Frost's mom had the girls. They were alone. Frost and Zep had made breakfast side by side after sleeping in. Zep couldn't explain it, but Frost felt distant—like his thoughts were elsewhere. No matter how hard Zep tried to make Frost smile, it never stuck for long. All day, the tension grew, killing Zep's plan to finally tell Frost he loved him while he had the chance. Zep had this speech prepared in his mind where he confessed his love and opened the discussion to them becoming one household, but Frost's mood was choking the life from Zep. Unfortunately, Zep had a bad feeling he knew why Frost wasn't himself, and his name was Scott. If one visit got in Frost's head like this, what would happen if Scott didn't back down? This was just one time of Scott asking Frost to come back. What would happen after the second? The fifth? Millie and Lily were meant to be Scott's kids. Zep was no one. He was just some guy who had come along later and fallen in love with this family. Zep was starting to think that Frost wouldn't choose him in the end if Scott kept coming around.

By the time Helena came through the door with the twins, it was almost a relief. Until she left and Millie cried for him to pick her up, that is. Her little body was on fire. Zep pressed his cheek to her forehead. "Holy crap, you're burning up." He met Frost's stare. Frost must have seen the fear in Zep's eyes.

He immediately moved to Zep's side and felt Millie's forehead before moving to her cheek. "Damn. Let me grab the thermometer."

Millie was lethargic and whiney as hell. Zep and Frost held each other's stare as they waited for the thermometer to beep. It seemed to take forever. It finally signaled its end.

Frost eyed the device. His gaze shot to Zep's. "One hundred and three. Holy shit, Zep. That's high. She's never had a fever this high. Do you mind keeping Lily while I take her to the hospital?"

Zep made a calming gesture as Frost took Millie

from his arms, trying to get Frost to take a breath. "Kids are resilient as hell, Frost. Let's give her some Motrin first and then some Tylenol in about four fours. We could even call her doctor while we wait. If that doesn't work, then maybe head to the ER. My guess is it's just a virus. There's nothing they can do for a virus at the ER. Plus, that place is full of germs."

"Will you or won't you watch Lily?" Frost asked, switching from panicked to pissed in an instant.

Zep didn't get a chance to respond. The doorbell rang. Zep swallowed a growl. He didn't get a vote here, but he didn't think taking Millie out in the rain to sit in the waiting room for hours, with people who had god only knew what, was the answer. "I'll get that." He didn't wait for Frost to respond before heading for the door. With any luck, it was Frost's mom returning. She could help him calm Frost's fears. A guy styled to perfection stood on the other side of the door.

Zep fought a spike of irritation. Now wasn't the time. "No one is looking for Jesus here." He tried shutting the door.

The guy put his hand out, stopping the door from closing. "I'm here for Frost."

Frost ran around behind Zep, gathering jackets and shoes they had just removed from the girls. "I don't have time for this right now, Scott. Millie needs to go to the ER."

Scott shoved his way inside, looking surprisingly concerned. "Why? What's wrong?"

"She has a high fever."

This was Scott? Anger flared to life in Zep's chest. "Frost said now isn't the time."

Scott barely spared him a glance. "Mind your business. Our daughter is sick."

Zep couldn't believe his ears. "Frost's daughter is sick, and you need to go."

Frost had a girl in each arm as he headed for the door. "By all means, fight amongst yourselves. I have to go."

Zep lost his patience. "Would you wait a damn minute, Frost? I don't think she needs to go to the hospital, but if you're determined—"

Frost spun on him with so much fury in his eyes that Zep took a step back. "You're not a real doctor and these aren't your kids. Stay out of it."

Before Zep recovered from the shock of Frost's sudden attack, Frost was out the door. Scott was on his heels, helping Frost leave Zep behind. They disappeared out the back door and into the garage. Zep stood there with the front door wide open and his heart beating in his ears. He had no clue what happened, but he was pretty sure—in a moment of panic—Frost had made his choice. He had chosen Scott.

Frost couldn't stop tapping his foot and bobbing his knee, waiting for the doctor to show. They had been waiting for hours while Scott stared at him relentlessly. Frost's arms were numb from holding his sleeping girls. Scott hadn't offered to help. Hell would freeze before Frost accepted, but he couldn't stop himself from comparing Scott's every action to Zep's. He should have waited for Zep to come with him. Zep would never let Frost do all this by himself. Frost was just fucking scared as hell. He would die if anything happened to one of his babies. If Zep had come, not only would he be helping with the girls, he would have made sure Frost didn't internally panic for six hours. Frost still wasn't sure how Scott even ended up here. One second, Frost had been strapping the kids in their car seats. The next, Scott had been climbing into the passenger seat. Frost was too panicked to fight with him.

"Who was that guy at the house?"

Frost didn't bother looking Scott's way. "My boyfriend."

"Really?"

At Scott's disbelieving tone, Frost shot him an irritated look. "He's a good man."

"Really?"

Frost took a steadying breath. He did not need this right now. "You should get a cab to take you back to your car. I'll likely be here a lot longer."

"In a minute. Let's revisit the fact that you're not only dating a biker daddy, you're also bringing him around my kids."

Frost could barely breathe. He wanted to lose his shit, but he couldn't, because unlike Scott, he had responsibilities. "These aren't your kids. They're mine. In fact, Zep could argue they're more his kids than they'll ever be yours. He's the one who's been here."

"Dada."

Frost's heart turned over in his chest at Millie's voice. She sounded like her throat hurt. He found himself making a shushing sound. Even he didn't know if it was directed at her, Scott, or himself. "It's okay, baby. I've got you."

"I want daddy Zep."

Even though Frost felt certain she had only

gotten her words twisted while asking for Zep, his heart rose to his throat. Zep should be there with them, but Frost had shut him out. He didn't want Scott here. His mind had been such a mess since yesterday. Scott had always fucked with his head.

"So they're calling this guy Dad now?"

"Please leave."

Scott stood with such force, his chair banged into the wall. Millie started crying. Frost thought he might too.

"Call me when this is over. We need to talk."

Frost didn't respond. He couldn't. Scott wanted to talk when this was over. As if Millie's emergency was an inconvenience for him. Her illness stood in the way of them working things out. Just like her existence had driven Scott away almost three years ago. Everything hurt. Frost wanted Zep.

The door opened and an elderly man in a lab coat stepped inside. He barely spared Millie a glance. "Her bloodwork is fine. It's likely just a virus. Rotate Motrin and Tylenol every four hours and make sure she stays hydrated. Follow up with her pediatrician in the morning."

Frost barely thanked the man before he was gone again. Defeat weighed heavily on Frost's shoulders as he made his way back to the car. Six hours at the ER only to learn what Zep had already told him.

Both girls were crying now. They were likely starving. With no energy left to spare, he ran through a drive thru and grabbed them a couple of kid's meals and let them eat in the car. He heard a drink spill. Frost was too tired to care. No one cried, so he assumed they were both asleep and the mess in his backseat was likely legendary.

Thankfully, Scott's car was gone, but Zep's truck wasn't. Frost pushed the food aside and carried the girls straight to bed before going in search of Zep. He found him sitting in the dark in the den.

"You were right. It's likely just a virus."

Zep stood and grabbed his shoes. "That's great. I'm glad she'll be okay." Zep sat and put on his shoes.

"Wait. Are you leaving?"

Zep's shoulders expanded as if he took a deep breath. He didn't quite meet Frost's eyes, and Frost knew. They were over. "I've been sitting here thinking while you were gone, and I've come to terms with some things I've been trying to ignore. I've spent the last six months falling in love with you and falling in love with your girls. All the while, you've spent the last six months waiting for us to be done."

The lump in Frost's throat grew. "That's not

true. I don't want to lose you. Things just got crazy tonight."

Zep finally met his stare. "You left here with Scott."

Frost tried to work up the energy to defend himself. "So you're leaving because he jumped in the car with me when I didn't have the luxury of fighting with him."

A sad smile touched Zep's lips. He stood. "No, baby. I'm not. I'm leaving because you don't really want a life with me, and I can't keep pretending that you do. I don't know if you still want Scott or if you're still so enraged by what he did that you can't let me in. Either way, you're not free to be with me. The longer I stay, the more it'll hurt when you tell me to go."

Frost knew there had to be some words he could say to make Zep stay, but he couldn't find them. Then Zep finished him.

"I love you." Zep's eyes filled with tears as if his heart was breaking. "And I love your girls. Please don't..." Zep shook his head, as if realizing anything he said at this point would be unfair. "I hope you have a wonderful life." Without a backward glance, Zep walked away. Frost stared at the spot where Zep had been waiting all night. He was mentally and physically exhausted. All he wanted was to curl up in Zep's arms and rest. Once again, life had slapped him back into his place. Frost moved to the couch and dropped. He had nothing left to give. Maybe tomorrow, he would know where he had gone wrong. Tonight, he just felt tired.

EIGHT

EVERYTHING WAS A HAZE. The room spun just a little. Zep was damn glad Kit had talked him into getting shit-faced while sitting at a table in the corner of Road Clan bar rather than at a barstool. He usually liked sitting at the bar. Drinks came faster that way. Lucky worked the taps tonight. Since they were friends and everyone knew Frost had crushed him, Lucky kept the drinks coming all night.

Unfortunately, the more Zep drank, the darker his thoughts turned. He had been such a fool for thinking someone as sexy as Frost could possibly want him. Zep didn't have low self-esteem, but he also wasn't blind. Frost looked like a man who made a living from working on his body. Zep liked being his age, and food. What an idiot he had been with

Frost. He couldn't stop having that thought, over and over again. For real, why had he thought he was special? Frost had been sleeping with men like Damon, for fuck's sake. Even though Damon was their age, he had a very god-like physique. Zep was an idiot.

Kit reached over and stroked his arm. He was the one person who never let Zep down. All night, he had sat at Zep's side without a single "I told you so" while staying sober so he could drive. Zep wished he could just fall in love with Kit. At least Kit was loyal.

"We should get married."

Kit flashed him a sympathetic smile. "You don't want me, sweetie. I don't like kids that much."

Because he knew Kit would never take him seriously, Zep didn't stop. "I'd take good care of you."

"I know."

A lump formed in Zep's throat. "I really thought he was the one."

Kit nodded. "I know."

Zep scooped Kit from his seat and pulled him into his lap. When Kit wrapped his arms around Zep's neck, a tear rolled down Zep's cheek. He hated himself for being so blind and stupid. Everything felt emptier now than before he had known what he was missing. Kit was his friend. Sometimes, he forgot why, but tonight Kit reminded him how amazing he could be when the chips were down.

"Daddy?"

Zep swallowed past the lump. He knew Kit really thought of him that way. That was the real reason Zep never stopped taking care of him. Kit needed him. "Yes, baby."

"You'll always have me."

More tears escaped. "I know."

Kit kissed his temple and whispered against his skin. "Frost has no idea what he and his girls lost. I wish like hell you had rescued me sooner."

Zep sucked in an unsteady breath and held Kit tighter. Thankfully, Kit had positioned him facing the wall long before the alcohol hit. It was bad enough that he couldn't stop the tears leaking from his eyes without people also looking at him.

Kit kissed his ear. "I'll stay with you tonight. You won't be alone."

Another set of traitorous thoughts creeped in. Who would be with Frost? Were the girls okay? It had only been one night. Was Millie any better today? He had to keep reminding himself that they weren't his kids. Still, this wasn't fair to them. He shouldn't have come into their lives. They wouldn't understand. Frost's face as Zep had left kept flaring to life in Zep's mind, making him wonder if he had made a mistake. Zep had never questioned himself as much as he had since Frost. There had been many times in his life when he had made enormous changes with massive consequences. When it came to Frost, Zep just didn't know if he had made the right decision this time. He had wanted so hard to believe they were real. Zep no longer knew his own mind. He kissed Kit's shoulder. This was reality. Frost had been a dream. He just needed a few more drinks, and then maybe he would forget. Otherwise, Zep had no clue how to survive losing Frost. He didn't know if he wanted to.

From the doorway at Road Clan, Frost watched Zep holding and kissing Kit. Even though he knew it was platonic, Frost's feet wouldn't budge. Maybe anyone else would have looked at the scene and flown into a jealous rage, but Frost knew Zep. Zep was loyal to the depths of his soul, and Kit was more like a son to him. It was pure unadulterated pain and an inability to grasp how to fix things that kept Frost from approaching Zep. He didn't understand how he had broken them.

That it made it damn hard to know how to make it better.

"You're no longer welcome here. Consider yourself banned."

Frost tore his gaze away from Zep and focused on an enraged Damon. A tired-sounding breath escaped him. He wished he could say this was the first time Damon had looked at him this way. Unfortunately, it seemed like this was the only emotion he stirred in anyone any longer. "That's fair."

A deep line snapped between the giant ginger's eyebrows. "Why in the hell are you here if that's all you have to say?"

Without thinking, Frost's gaze slid back Zep's way. Why had he come here? Being here fixed nothing. It only tortured Frost with the sight of Zep's arms around someone else. No matter the reasons for Kit being in Zep's lap, Frost was the one who wanted the comfort he knew only Zep could give.

"No reason, I guess." Even to his ears, Frost sounded dead. He didn't wait for Damon to physically toss him out. Frost walked away. With years and maturity, Frost saw a lot of things more clearly now. Scott was one of those things. Frost had been young when he had been seduced by a mature man in a position of power. Ultimately, he had retired in the prime of his career for a fake dream. Nonetheless, Frost stood no chance of making things right with Zep until he faced the first man who broke him.

Frost straddled his Harley and headed across town. He had always known where to find Scott. Frost just never had a reason to go looking before now. When Scott had left, Frost had believed it was forever. There was no going back to someone who cheated. Maybe someone better than him could forgive that, but Frost wasn't that guy. He knew himself well enough to know things would never be the same. Frost didn't want to be miserable for the rest of his life, always wondering where Scott was or who he talked to on the phone. Was he playing games on his phone or texting another man? Frost couldn't live like that. Not that any of those reasons mattered. Frost was in love with Zep. No one else would do.

By the time he pulled into Scott's circular drive, in front of a house twice the size of Frost's expensive home, Frost knew what to do. He had to handle this now, and for good. He couldn't have Scott popping up every few years, ruining his life.

The roar of his Harley or the sight of him on the

security cameras must have brought Scott to the door. Whatever the reason, he stepped outside and sat on the front steps, waiting for Frost to meet him there.

Frost didn't hurry. He didn't want to face Scott. Frost hated that Scott still looked amazing, but he knew Scott was ugly where it counted most. Scott's true face was the only one Frost saw anymore.

Frost held his helmet against his body, trying to hide the way his hands shook. He didn't know if it was anger or nerves. Likely, it was both. He had never been good at fighting with Scott. That hadn't changed. The fact that Scott intimidated him should have been a warning bell several years ago. It was too late to turn back, and Frost wouldn't back down now. He had too much at stake.

"I don't want you to come around me or my girls again. You made your choice when you left."

For a long moment, Scott stared at him in silence. His expression gave nothing away. "You're not the same man as you were when we were together."

That was true. "I have responsibilities now."

Scott's stare didn't waver. "No. You're bitter. I'm surprised Zep hasn't run for the hills. He must be a great guy if he can see past this wall you've built."

An exasperated growl escaped Frost. "It's your

fault. You did this to me. Because of you, I have sabotaged every good thing to happen to me since you left. You have a lot of nerve, coming back and calling me bitter. It's your fucking fault."

To Frost's irritation, Scott never batted an eyelash. "I'm sorry, but it's not." Scott kept talking like there was no possibility Frost would kill him. "You're right that I did a terrible thing to you, but you chose how to react to it. You are one of the sexiest men alive. Why would you let anything I do make you less? You should have been out there fucking everything that moves until you felt like you'd shown me."

Frost wanted to pull out his hair. "It's like you never knew me at all. I don't want to fuck everyone. I want a quiet, steady life with a good man."

For a moment, Scott stared at him in silence. "Then maybe you don't know me either because I thought you knew I didn't want that. Yet, you still started planning kids without ever asking my feelings. For a while, I thought I could indulge you, but I couldn't. Why are you so angry with me? I told you time and time again that I was selfish and wanted you to myself. It was like you couldn't hear me—like you thought you could just force me to want to be a dad. Now I want to try to be who you want and who the girls need, but you're still mad all over again. Fuck, Frosty. Who are you really pissed off at? Me or you? Because it sounds like you don't want to be happy."

Maybe some of that was true, except for the parts that mattered now. "I want to be happy, but not with you. Zep loves me and he loves our kids. Not your kids. Mine and Zep's kids. He's the one who showed up and wanted to be there. Like you said, this was never the life you wanted. I should have heard that when you said it back then and set you free. I won't play deaf again. You don't want this life. Zep does. Don't come around again."

Scott's gaze dropped to the ground. He gave a subtle nod before meeting Frost's stare again. "For what it's worth, and despite every horrible mistake I made, you were always the one. Maybe in another life."

Frost had no response to that. He headed back for his bike. There would be no meeting Scott in another life. Zep was his soul mate. He would keep finding Zep again in every life, even if Zep was done with him in this one. Frost would be goddamned if Zep gave up on him if he could help it, though. Not if Frost had anything to say about it.

He drove the two blocks to Zep's, determined to

wait for him there. Frost got there just in time to see Kit heading inside alone. Kit turned at the sound of Frost's motorcycle. To his surprise, Kit waited for him. Of course, Frost imagined Kit planned to let him have it... again. It was like Kit's work was never done where Frost was concerned.

"He isn't here."

Frost drew a steadying breath. He wondered who Zep had gone home with, if not Kit. "Damn." Even though the curse had been under his breath, Frost swore it sounded loud as hell beneath Kit's disapproving stare. Frost started back toward his bike. He didn't know what to do now.

"FYI, Zep is a real doctor, you know." Frost turned at Kit's words. Kit sat on the front steps and focused on Frost. "He left a lucrative OBGYN practice to help women who preferred to have their babies outside the traditional hospital setting, but he still has his medical license. Also, he may not be Millie and Lily's dad—like you—but he loves your daughters and he's the guy who showed up. Also, you're a fucking idiot."

He was. It wasn't like Frost could argue.

A moment passed in silence. "So why are you here?"

"Because I love him."

Kit rolled his eyes. "Of course you do, he's fucking lovable. That doesn't answer my question. Why are you here?"

For a moment, Frost felt the overwhelming urge to throw his helmet as far as he could and scream at the top of his lungs. He didn't get to throw tantrums. It seemed like he was the only one. "I have to make things right, even though I have no fucking clue what I did wrong."

"You didn't do anything wrong."

That brought Frost up short. He stared at Kit in silence.

Kit shrugged. "Unless you count being ungodly sexy and already having the life Zep desperately wants as a bad thing, then you did everything wrong."

Frost's eyebrows drew closer together as his confusion grew.

Kit released a loud sigh. "Come on, Frost. You had to know Zep is a squishy teddy bear who is easily crushed. He needs hugs, kisses, and reassurance that he's the one you want forever and ever, because you have everything he wants in life and he thinks he has nothing to offer someone like you."

"What do you mean, someone like me?"

An adorable growl escaped Kit. "Goddamn,

Frost. Do you even own a mirror? You're amazing on the outside. Personally, I'm not so sure about the inside, but you have Zep's attention and he's a pretty good judge of character. After all, he's sees past my bullshit. That's a fucking feat."

"He says you're a rambutan."

To Frost's surprise, Kit's mouth snapped shut at his claim. Kit blinked rapidly, as if he fought a sudden wave of tears. He visibly swallowed. "He deserves better than you."

"I know."

"But you're who he loves."

For a moment, Frost wondered if he would be the one who cried. "I know."

"I dropped him off at your office because you weren't home. He's determined to wait for you and make you see that he's the one who deserves you. Not Scott. I couldn't talk him out of it. He's pretty drunk."

Frost bit his bottom lip, trying not to smile. "He's lucky to have you."

"Damn fucking skippy and don't you forget it. We are a package deal."

Frost quickly jogged up the steps and kissed Kit's cheek. "Go to bed. Brush your teeth. All those fatherly statements. He won't be home tonight."

"Yeah, yeah." Kit gave Frost's chest a pat. "You're marrying my dad. I get it. Get lost."

Frost snorted. "I love you too."

Kit didn't quite meet Frost's gaze, giving Frost the freedom to look at him closer than usual. Frost realized Kit had been crying at some point tonight, and he didn't look as catty as his tone always suggested. In fact, he looked incredibly young and vulnerable. The dad in Frost rose to the surface.

He stooped, leaving Kit no choice but to meet his stare. "Would you tell me if you needed me?"

Kit shrugged.

"I want you to. If you need me, I'm here. I know you don't know me like you know Zep, but I care."

Kit nodded. He swiped at his eyes. "I'm serious. Get lost. He's super drunk and I left him at your desk. I can't promise he won't puke in there."

Frost pressed another quick kiss to Kit's cheek. One day, he would pry Kit's story from Zep. He knew Zep saw something in Kit that Frost was only now starting to see. Without a backward glance, Frost headed for the gym. Apparently, Zep was waiting. Frost couldn't risk Zep drunkenly stumbling around town, searching for him. It was his turn to take care of Zep, the way Zep had been silently caring for Frost since they'd met.

WITH FROST'S OFFICE CHAIR BACKED AGAINST the corner of the filing cabinet, Zep settled in to wait. He tried not to let his gaze slide toward the pictures on Frost's desk. He couldn't let himself believe he would never see Millie and Lily again, but Frost might tell him to go fuck himself when he showed up. Zep had to tell himself Frost was working tonight. The only other option was that Frost was with Scott. Zep couldn't live with that. Frost belonged to him.

To keep from staring at the pictures, Zep closed his eyes. The room spun. He lifted his foot and braced it on the edge of the desk, hoping it would stop. Zep needed to get his shit together before Frost came back to his office. It was possible he had drunk too much. Fuck. He just wanted to be in bed with Frost. How had things gone so wrong so fast? He wanted their life back.

His head bobbed as if he had accidentally dozed off. Zep's eyes shot open. Frost sat across from him, watching him. Zep scrambled to sit up straight and pretend sobriety.

"Hi. I wasn't sleeping." Zep threw his arm out

and snagged the edge of the desk to steady himself when the room spun again.

"Would you like to be?"

"Yes. No. I don't know. What was the question?"

An adorable smile touched Frost's lips. "Come on, baby. You need some sleep. The girls never sleep in, so I have a feeling you'll regret tying this one on in the morning."

Zep couldn't stop blinking. He had no idea what was happening. He heard something about the girls, though. "How is Millie?"

"She's great. Woke up this morning, running around like nothing happened."

"Good. That's good." He tried to stand. The room spun again. "I think I need like some crackers or some water."

A soft, sexy-sounding chuckle rumbled from Frost. "The girls have some animal crackers and juice boxes in my desk. That's the best I can do."

A shot of pain hit Zep in the chest. "I can't take the babies' crackers and juice. What kind of man gets drunk and steals food from kids?" He grabbed his head, trying to force himself sober. "It's no wonder you want Scott over me. I bet he doesn't steal the girls' food."

Frost sat on the edge of the desk in front of Zep.

Zep hadn't realized Frost was so close. He looked beautiful. "Is that what you think? That I want Scott over you?"

Zep gestured wildly. It was like he couldn't control his arms. "Well, yeah. I mean, you're you and he's him and I'm me. He's a piece of shit, but you trust him and not me. It's like, not fair and shit." His shoulders fell in defeat.

"Look at me."

Zep thought that he was, but Frost snapped his fingers and Zep's gaze shot to Frost's face, so maybe he hadn't been.

Frost looked serious. "I love you. Our girls love you. You are the only man I want for the rest of my life. Scott doesn't deserve to breathe the same air as you. No way do I want him near Lily and Millie. Are you listening?"

"Yes."

Frost smiled. "What did I say?"

"Scott sucks and you love me."

Another sexy chuckle fell from Frost's lips. "Close enough."

"I don't think I can walk right now. The room is spinning and stuff. But if I could, I would kiss you and tell you I love you too."

"Baby, you don't need to be able to walk to tell me you love me too."

Zep blinked. That made sense. "Oh. I love you too."

A blinding smile lit Frost's face. "I'm really not sure how much of this you'll remember in the morning."

Zep shrugged. "I've never been so drunk that I couldn't recall what I've done. Any guy who tells you that is full of shit and only trying to get away with something." Some of those words might have been slurred. Zep couldn't tell. "My legs may not work, but my brain is fine."

"What about your lips? Do those work?" Frost made a dismissive motion before Zep could answer. "Never mind. I can find out for myself." Frost swooped in and whisked his lips across Zep's in a light kiss. "Don't ever leave me again."

Zep stared at Frost's lips as he nodded. "I won't. Promise."

Frost sucked Zep's bottom lip between his teeth and nibbled. "I'll need more than a promise from you. The last twenty-four hours have been hell. I'm going to need you to come off a little more than just your word." He buried his face against Zep's neck and kissed.

Zep's eyes fell closed as goosebumps rose on his skin. "Tell me what you need. It's yours."

"You'll have to move in with me, first off. I get that means setting up a bedroom for Kit too. We'll give him one of the upstairs rooms and talk to him about not bringing strange men home where our daughters live."

He liked that Frost kept calling the girls theirs, but he couldn't let Frost think that about Kit. "Kit doesn't bring home men. Despite his constant flirting, he doesn't like to be touched sexually." His brain caught up with his mouth. "I probably shouldn't have told you that."

Frost leaned away and peeled off his shirt, giving Zep one of his favorite views. "It's fine. I won't tell. Are you good so far?"

Zep stared at Frost's body and nodded. "Yep. Keep going."

Frost unbuttoned and unzipped his pants. "I think, to be safe, you should probably marry me and adopt the girls. We don't want any misunderstandings in the future about who belongs to whom."

While Zep was definitely distracted by the way Frost slipped his hand inside his pants, teasing Zep with an upcoming show, Frost's words had his attention. Zep's gaze snapped to Frost's face. He looked serious. "Is that really what you want?"

Frost bit his lip as his hand kept moving inside his pants. "Do you really plan to make me repeat myself or do you plan to make them legs work so you can fuck me?"

Whoa. Zep had no idea how he had gotten so lucky. This unbelievably sexy man wanted to marry Zep and share his children with him. Topping all that, he never hesitated to do any hot as hell act to keep Zep in line.

"If there are condoms and lube in this room, I have some fucking questions."

Frost laughed at Zep's jealousy. "Come on, sexy bear. You know there are plenty of ways to have sex without penetration. Plus, I just asked you to marry me. Are you planning on clinging to condoms for the rest of our lives?"

Zep had already lost some threads of the conversation. A wave of overwhelming happiness washed over him. "I can't believe we're getting married. You're so beautiful. No one will believe you're mine."

"Focus, Bear. I'm trying to seduce you."

Zep tried scrambling to his feet. He was ready to be seduced. His legs didn't support his weight, but the chair rolled. Zep decided to take what he could get. He rolled the chair until he could snag Frost's waist and tow him closer.

"Stop teasing. I want a taste." Zep shoved Frost's hand aside and licked Frost's erection. "Goddamn. You taste good. You should take off your pants."

Instead of doing as Zep asked, Frost grabbed the first aid kit. He popped open the box and came out with a white packet. Frost winked at him. "No need for questioning. Most first aid kits have lube in them. I've never known why."

Zep found his footing. He was about to fuck this sexy guy who would soon be married to him. Zep snagged the pack from Frost's fingers as he came to his feet. "Lube is sterile, so it's the first line of defense against infections where there's chafing or minor cuts."

"Right. Doctor. Forgot."

With Frost this close and half dressed, Zep felt suddenly sober. "Pants, John Michael."

Frost chuckled. "Oooh. Both my first names. I am in trouble." He pushed his pants down his hips. Zep claimed Frost's mouth. He couldn't stand not having Frost's tongue stroking his. Zep went to work on the front of his pants, setting his erection free. Proving he wasn't fully sober, things seemed to happen in snatches. One second, they were kissing. The next, Frost coated Zep's dick in lube. Zep turned Frost in his arms and led his hands to the desk. He kissed Frost's shoulder as he ran the backs of his knuckles down Frost's spine.

"You are a work of art." He flattened his palm against the small of Frost's back. Frost widened his stance. Zep swiped his crown up and down Frost's crack, teasing them both. "I don't deserve you," he admitted as he impaled Frost with his cock. "But you're still mine."

A loud moan filled the air, bouncing off the walls of the tiny office. Frost's tight heat sucked him deeper. Zep's eyes fell closed. He savored every sensation of being inside the man he loved. Everything had a surreal edge with so much alcohol pumping through his veins. He thrust, letting Frost's moans guide him.

"Anyone walking by can hear you."

Frost pushed back against him, taking what he wanted. "I don't care. Let them listen."

The idea of an audience sent Zep's lust through the roof. He wasn't dumb. Zep knew Frost was way out of his league. For whatever reason, though, Frost had fallen in love with him. Everyone should know it. Zep thrust harder. Frost covered his own mouth to muffle his cries. Every sound Frost made drove Zep insane. He lost control, thrusting hard and fast. The sound of skin slapping joined the sound of Frost's barely muted moans.

Zep didn't try to be quiet. "That's it. Let me hear your pleasure. I want everyone here to know you're mine. You belong to me." Zep slowed long enough to kiss Frost's shoulder. He thrust hard at the right angle. "Tell them who owns you."

"Oh my god, Zep. Do that again."

Zep didn't need to be told twice. He held tight to Frost and pounded the spot he needed. Frost's muscles tensed. Zep held his breath. Frost slammed himself back so hard on Zep's dick that Zep saw stars. Frost cried out. His body convulsed, sucking an orgasm from Zep—like stealing his soul. Zep whimpered against Frost's back as wave after wave of ecstasy rocked him. Reality didn't creep in. It hit Zep like a brick. His hands shook as he tilted Frost's face his way for a kiss. He couldn't believe this amazing guy had proposed to him. Maybe it had been more like a demand. Semantics. They were getting married. This would always be his life. He squeezed Frost so tightly to his chest that Frost gasped. Zep had to force himself to loosen his hold.

"I love you." Zep couldn't say it enough to

appease his soul. "I'm going to spoil the fuck out of you."

A tired-sounding chuckle burst from Frost. "I love you too and you already do. I believe in us."

Zep did too. That was why he had argued with Kit and threatened to walk here if he had to, doing and saying whatever it took to get Kit to bring him here tonight. Maybe it had taken a lot of alcohol to see past himself, but Zep believed in them. He had decided if Scott wanted Frost, he would have to fight for him. Zep didn't intend to give in easily. They were meant to be. Everything else was just noise. Frost wasn't getting rid of him. They were forever.

NINE

IT WASN'T that Kit didn't like kids as much as he had never been around them. His childhood had been something straight out of a nightmare. He had grown up, chosen to be fabulous, and never thought about being helpless again. When Zep had done the quickie marriage thing, locking Frost down as fast as possible, Kit could have gone on his way. He had never done well on his own. It wasn't that he couldn't afford his own place. Kit wasn't good at being alone. So Kit had graciously accepted Frost and Zep's offer to continue on as he had been, crashing with Zep. This left him in the odd position of having coffee with toddlers each morning.

At first, he had tried simply ignoring the twins. Gah. He didn't understand why such sticky creatures had to be so cute. Kit had always been an early riser. He found himself more and more often spending the early morning hours with the girls so Zep could sleep. Kit told himself he bore the weight of this chore because Zep delivered a lot of middle-of-the-night babies. He lived here for free. The least he could do was watch the girls occasionally. But damn, he adored them. The way he felt ready to kill anyone who dared to harm them made his own childhood all that much worse upon reflection. Kit got the feeling his reaction to them was normal. He never dreamed anything about himself would be the least bit well-adjusted. Who knew?

Matthew came through the back door, as if he lived there too. Kit tried ignoring his beauty—the way he always did. The problem was that Matthew was impossible to ignore. He looked like the yoga instructor he was. Tight, trim body. Shaggy light brown hair. Tattoos on every inch of skin, as far as Kit had seen. Only his face had been spared, which was a good thing, because that was a work of art. Hazel eyes. Just yum. He made Kit wish he wasn't such a mess, but he was, so there was that.

"Are you ready to go to lunch?"

Kit finished tying Lily's shoes. "Almost. I need to drop these two at their grandma's house. Zep didn't get home from work until an hour ago. He needs his sleep."

Matthew stooped and the girls launched themselves at him. His infectious smile showed exactly how comfortable he was with the twins. He took turns kissing sticky cheeks. "That's cool. Me and these chicks get along just fine."

Kit blew out a sigh. There was no one Matthew couldn't charm. Honestly, Kit had no clue why Matthew kept coming back for more of Kit's rejection.

Matthew helped him move car seats and get the girls strapped in. At Helena's, he flirted and teased, making Helena smile and blush. All the while, Kit barely heard a word. His attention was locked on Matthew. Not for the first time, Kit wondered what it must be like to be him. Most people considered Kit beautiful. In fact, he got paid to be pretty. Once people got past Kit's looks, they realized what Kit knew every second of every day. He wasn't likable. Matthew was adored by everyone.

The moment they were alone inside Kit's SUV, Matthew turned sideways in his seat, staring at Kit as he drove. "Tell me something about you no one knows."

"No thank you." Kit didn't try softening the rejection with a smile.

Matthew didn't seem bothered. "Come on, Kit. We've been going to lunch together a few times a week for almost a year now and I feel like I still don't know you at all."

Kit stopped at a red light and looked Matthew's way. "I once killed a man for asking too many questions."

Matthew laughed. Even that was sexy and engaging. He patted Kit's knee. Kit fought the urge to hiss like an angry cat. "Just wait, Kitty. One of these days, you'll tell me all your deepest and darkest secrets. I'm persistent. You can't shake me by giving me the cold shoulder. The harder the shell, the sweeter the fruit."

A snort escaped Kit, but he also couldn't stop smiling. This was how Matthew did it. This was how he kept Kit coming back for more. Maybe one day Matthew would break down his walls. He would likely run for the hills once he saw the mess underneath, but Kit liked Matthew. He thought Matthew might really like him too. Truthfully, Matthew scared Kit a little. There was something slightly dark about him—like he had a side of him that no one saw, but Kit caught glimpses of it when

Matthew wasn't looking. Sometimes, Kit thought, maybe he should be the one to run. He had no idea why he couldn't. For whatever reason, whatever Matthew hid, Kit felt safer with him than he did anyone else, even Zep. Maybe that was the most frightening part of all.

FROST KISSED ZEP'S NECK, SELFISHLY HOPING TO wake him. He knew Zep had been working all night and he tried to let Zep sleep, but they didn't have the girls for the night. Frost wanted a little time alone with his husband.

"Paging Dr. Frost."

Zep's eyes didn't open, but his lips shaped a smile.

Frost worked a little harder. "I love my sleepy bear."

"I love you too."

A smile exploded across Frost's face at Zep's grumbled voice. "I know you want to hibernate. I'll go take a shower so you can have a few more minutes."

One arm shot out and curled around Frost, keeping him pinned to the bed. "No. Mine."

Frost couldn't stop smiling. When the twins had been born, Frost had stared at them in wonder. He hadn't realized it was possible to love anyone as much as he did his children. Then he fell in love with Zep, and he realized real love was supposed to feel like this. They were unbreakable. No fights or anger were permanent here. Their love was too strong.

Zep squirmed closer until Frost was tucked against him. "There. You don't leave me." He sounded like a baby, making Frost's smile grow. Life felt perfect. It felt like the right time to talk.

"Let's have another baby."

Zep's eyes finally opened. The hope in his expression kept Frost charging forward with something he had been thinking about since they married.

"We have two daughters. Let's try for a son. I'd love to have a little boy with your hair and eyes." He thought for a second. "Or another little girl. I don't care. We should have more kids."

Frost knew Zep well enough to know when he tried to temper his reaction. He definitely held back now. "I work the perfect profession for finding someone to carry our baby. I doubt Lori wants to do it twice."

Frost tried not to jump up and down on the bed. "I don't know. After the girls were born, she said she would be open to doing it again. She says she likes being pregnant and it was worth it to see the way I look at them. It's possible she would do it again."

Zep bit his bottom lip, visibly fighting a smile. "So, are we really doing this?"

Frost nodded. "I want more."

A happy-sounding shout assaulted Frost's ears before Zep pounced. He pinned Frost to the bed and kissed every place he could reach. Tears pressed at backs of Frost's eyes unexpectedly. This was what he had been missing the first time around. Scott was right. Frost hadn't wanted to hear that Scott didn't want kids. He had barreled ahead, having the twins with no concern for Scott's feelings. Frost regretted nothing. He wanted a house full of children. The fact that Scott didn't should have been Frost's first clue that Scott wasn't the one for him. Now he understood what it was like to have someone else feel the same. He knew Zep loved the twins, but this was a bit different. Zep would be there from day one. They would bring a baby home together.

Zep swiped at his eyes, and Frost realized his big softy was crying.

"Oh, baby. I love you. Why are you crying?"

Zep shook his head. "I never thought I would find you."

Frost's vision blurred. If he was being honest, he never thought he would find Zep either. He didn't think anyone would put him first and love him the way Zep did. "Thank god you did."

Zep buried his face in the crook of Frost's neck and held on. Frost held him every bit as tight. The first time he had looked into his daughters' eyes, he had known miracles were real. Frost never expected Zep would show him that miracles happened more often than he could ever dream. He couldn't wait to see what happened next. Frost knew it would be amazing.

Keep an eye out for the next Candied Crush, *Beautifully Explosive*.

Please consider leaving a review at the retailer where you purchased this book. Reviews really help with a book's visibility, which allows me to continue writing more stories. Thank you, Charity.

ABOUT THE AUTHOR

Charity Parkerson is an award-winning and multi-published author with several companies. Born with no filter from her brain to her mouth, she decided to take this odd quirk and insert it in her characters.

*Eight-time Readers' Favorite Award Winner
　　*2015 Passionate Plume Award Finalist
　　*2013 Reviewers' Choice Award Winner
　　*2012 ARRA Finalist for Favorite Paranormal Romance
　　*Five-time winner of The Mistress of the Darkpath

Connect with her online:

—Sign up for my newsletter: http://bit.ly/CharityNews
　　—Join my readers' group on Facebook: http://bit.ly/CharitysTribe
　　—Website: charityparkerson.com

—Facebook: facebook.com/authorCharityParkerson

facebook.com/TheMenofSin

—Twitter: twitter.com/CharityParkerso

—Instagram: Instagram.com/sinnerauthor

—Bookbub: https://www.bookbub.com/authors/charity-parkerson

—Amazon page: author.to/CharityParkerson

www.ingramcontent.com/pod-product-compliance
Lightning Source LLC
Chambersburg PA
CBHW060233180626
46813CB00007B/3062